THE DUKE'S LAST WORD

LOVE, MOST ARDENTLY

BOOK ONE

SOPHIE LEIGH FOX

eBook ISBN: 979-8-9901281-0-1

print ISBN: 979-8-9901281-2-5

For Marlay

PROLOGUE

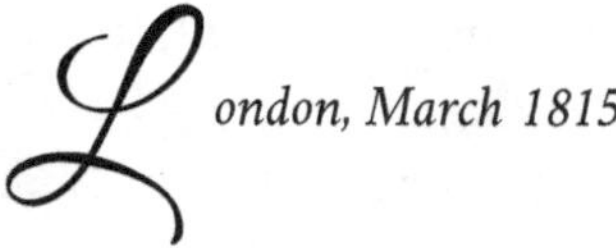 *ondon, March 1815*

JAMES FRANCIS BARROW, Duke of Heighbury, met the older man's wrinkled hand with a firm shake.

Four of James's companions clapped him on the back. "Congratulations!"

His jubilant smile curdled into the briefest of frowns.

Had James made a terrible mistake? Should he have let the old man pay his debt instead of offering to settle it for him?

"Well, now that is done. Let us celebrate with some cheer." Sir Edgar Middleton raised a trembling finger to signal another round, but James caught the man's wrist.

"I think we've done enough celebrating, sir. If we do much more, we won't have any left in us for the actual event."

The man bobbed his head, slowed by too many pints. "Capital, capital. I will expect the papers to me in the next week. You shall come to Middleton Grange thereafter and meet my daughter."

James readily agreed and downed the rest of his ale.

"You lucky dog, you've outdone yourself this time. Just think, not only do you save your inheritance and increase your estate with a fine piece of land, but you gain a *filly* to seal the bargain," Sir Lawrence D'Arby of London, James's distant cousin on his father's side, interjected with a knowing smirk. His raucous laughter sent a warning through James's bones.

Shrugging off doubt, James assured Middleton that he'd be in touch soon and hailed the poor sop a carriage to carry him back to his London lodgings. When the hackney had disappeared into the London fog, James returned to the group and announced he'd also be leaving.

"Ho, there. Stay, and let's have some supper," D'Arby said, his black eyes brimming with amusement.

"Another time, perhaps." James wrapped his cloak around him and nearly reached the exit when his cousin stopped him.

"I'd say you've got yourself quite a bargain." D'Arby pressed his lips together and raised his eyebrows in typical fashion.

Only if Middleton's daughter agrees to be my wife.

He thought he might remember meeting the girl last spring at a ball. A quiet, unassuming beauty who seemed less pleased with her surroundings than other wallflowers waiting to fill dance cards. But time was running out. According to his late father's will, if the duke didn't marry by his thirtieth birthday, he would lose his inheritance to D'Arby and be unable to maintain his family estate of many generations.

"This is the last time I'll see you at these gaming tables. I refuse to be a party to such underhandedness." James had grown weary of D'Arby's surreptitious behavior in recent months.

D'Arby sneered. "Admit it, Cousin. You enjoy the fruits of your labor just as much as I do."

James shook his head. "Not in this manner." He set his jaw. Even he had morals when taking advantage of a drunken old gentleman whose lack of judgment nearly lost his estate to a swindler like D'Arby.

"Then why don't you run after the old fool and tell him it's off? I'll be happy to assume the debt. He did, after all, lose to me. You are far too kind to pay it for him. So long as you keep *your* part of the bargain to *me*." D'Arby's guffaw sent a bite up James's spine. "I see, Your Grace. You'd rather save your own hide than his. Admit it. Your morals are no different than mine." D'Arby slapped him on the back. "Look on the sunny side. You get the better of the pact anyhow, old chap. You get to marry the girl. Or would you prefer to trade places *again*?"

If he hadn't been under such good regulation, James would have set him a facer, like he had the day he discovered his then betrothed, Lady Genevieve Waterford of Brighton, in D'Arby's arms. Realizing that both parties deserved each other freed the duke from a miserable future. Her father, the Marquess of Hollingsworth, had discreetly released his daughter from the betrothal to save his family's reputation.

Instead of indulging D'Arby's remark with his fist, he closed the door behind him with a sharp click.

* * *

MIDDLETON'S HAND shook but not from the third glass of brandy. As he stared into the flames, his eyes glazed over; the paper detailing his contract with the duke crinkled in his gnarled hand.

The door to the study opened, and a familiar voice stirred him from his reverie.

"Papa?" His only daughter, Willa, approached and eased the crystal glass out of his grasp. "That's quite enough for tonight."

He nodded, offering a feeble smile. Blinking, he attempted to focus on the room.

So many memories from generations of family surrounded him. Tokens of travel to France and Ireland, books on adventures and education, and scents of leather and tobacco narrated a comfortable life as a country gentleman.

His great grandfather's portrait hung above the fireplace, staring down in judgment. Tears pricked his eyes, and he could no longer contain himself.

"My dear girl, we must have ourselves a chat."

"About what, Papa?"

The truth must come out. Middleton never wanted to place the responsibility on her delicate shoulders, but they were well past his pride. If the Grange were to be saved, she would be the solution.

He took her hands in his, a smile masking the melancholy in his heart.

"About your future."

CHAPTER 1

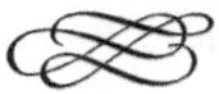

Surrey, Wednesday, April 19, 1815

My dearest Cassandra,

I have the most preposterous news. Whilst you are always the first to hear any news from the Grange, I have a devastating tale to share. Prepare yourself. There is no joy in these lines.

I fear my family has chosen my path for me. Papa has bargained me to a man without my consent, and Aunt Rosamunde has approved the transaction. If only my dear mama were still living to protect me from this most grievous blunder.

Papa has compromised our family estate, and I am the solution. This stranger to whom I have no temptation to meet, much less marry, will become the savior to Middleton Grange, but only if I consent to be his wife in but a fortnight.

If I accept the arrangement, Middleton Grange will be saved. If I refuse, we shall be destitute in mere months. How could Papa have been so reckless with our fortune? And why would a wealthy, titled man need more property and a wife far beneath his rank? Dearest Cassandra, my most beloved friend and confidante, pray, rescue me from this abomination before I am lost forever.

Wilhemina Rose Middleton sat at the writing table in her bedchamber, preparing the shocking update for her cousin. How she wished she could share the news in person, hiding beneath the bedcovers as they had in childhood. No matter the method of conveying the information, her life as she knew it was finished. Wilhemina sighed. The crackling of the fireplace was no longer a comfort but an ominous accent to the regrettable situation her papa had placed her in.

Laughter in the salon reached the tips of her ears, but the festive mood remained outside an invisible gate to her spirit.

How can I marry a stranger?

The goose quill in her hand quivered, and then the tremor grew more violent as rage bore within Wilhemina. If she were honest, it wasn't just anger that drove her extremities to shake. The bothersome trembling in her hands had come on recently, and she knew not why.

She pulled a loose mahogany curl from the knot at her nape until it unfurled into a limp strand. Inhaling, the aroma of her favorite tea from the untouched cup on her desk beckoned her. Instead of drinking the Bohea, she pressed on with her assignment to inform her cousin and closest confidante of the impending arrival of her doom. Or, as her father had arranged, her future bridegroom. She returned to the correspondence, determined to post the letter first thing tomorrow morn.

Papa has reminded me of no offers from last Season. Thus, he has sold me, his most dutiful daughter, to the highest bidder to marry me off as a stipulation to satisfy the gambling debt he owes the Duke of Heighbury. I had the unfortunate luck of being slighted by the man last spring at a ball. Being in London, you might have heard of him. He is known for his unsavory connections and behavior with ladies of the ton.

Willa paused. Reflecting on a singular balmy evening almost a year before, she remembered how his dark eyes had dismissed her in a modicum of consideration among a line of other debutantes. Perhaps she had not been a member of the upper society as most of the other young ladies. It offered a poor excuse for a proper gentleman to disregard any lady's presence–not to mention the gossip surrounding his broken engagement to a wealthy and respectable marquess's daughter.

Her fingers worried the gold cross she'd worn around her neck since the day tragedy struck their family, and death snatched her mama away in a senseless riding accident mere months before Willa's debut into society. Her vision blurred as tears rolled down her cheeks, but she refused to acknowledge them. If she were forced to endure a formal introduction to the man who casually snubbed her in a London ballroom, let her papa see her blotchy complexion, high from an effusion of tears. Let the duke drag her from her home, kicking and screaming in an unladylike manner. She would never behave so, but the thought of a rebellious act offered some unobtainable satisfaction in her mind.

She finished the letter to Cassandra, signing as Willa. A knock roused her from the daydream to flee her predicament. "Enter."

"Willa, dear, we are waiting for you. Won't you come down?" Her aunt, Rosamunde Livingston, swished across the room, her emerald gossamer dress stirring a breeze and sending the flames from the fireplace into a dance. "Dearest, why are you weeping so? This is the most blessed evening of your life. Well, second most, once you are married." She nudged Willa with her elbow, causing her niece to collapse on the writing table sobbing. "Come now. Stop dithering. Let's clean your face and make you presentable for your future husband," Rosamunde said as she tucked the wayward curl behind Willa's ear.

Accepting a handkerchief from her aunt, Willa dabbed her eyes and cheeks. Pride refused to allow her to cry in the man's presence, but she didn't mind overmuch if he saw the effects in her red, swollen eyes or splotchy cheeks. He was the intruder at Middleton Grange, not her.

She stopped in front of her looking glass. Dull hazel eyes met her with disapproval, their former fire having been extinguished.

Who are you, and what have you done with Wilhemina?

A week ago, she had been contented and carefree, never having to question the certainty of her future. Now, the man she was to marry was a guest in her house, and for Lord knows how long. She didn't mind being a spinster if it meant she could stay in her home forever as mistress of Middleton Grange. Why must life change?

"If we must, Aunt, let's get it over with. Though I'd rather have all my teeth pulled one by one."

Her aunt helped Willa into white kid gloves that once belonged to her late mother. Taking Willa's arm, she tucked it close. Patting her niece's hand, she reassured Willa that no teeth-pulling would be necessary. "I've just met him. I suspect you will like him well enough."

When Willa did not respond, her aunt continued. "My brother has compromised the estate, but the duke has provided the solution. So long as you agree to marry him, Middleton Grange will be saved. The thing has been done. Let's face it with dignity." Aunt Rosamunde tsked at her brother's folly. "You must accept it now with gratitude and be at ease that you will always have a home and financial security. And to be a duchess. This will make your father most happy."

"I cannot believe he would put me in such a horrid

predicament," Willa countered. "Why must a woman be ripped from her family and sanctuary only to be tossed about on a fishing line to the first eligible man? What about marrying for love?"

Her inclination toward the dramatic elicited a reprimand from her aunt. "My darling girl, it is well past time for you to have your own family. You've had two Seasons already." She took Willa's chin in hand and forced her gaze. "Many girls would give up a lot to be betrothed to a man of means and title. Do your papa proud and accept your future as a duchess. And behave like the dutiful daughter and lady your mama raised you to be."

As much of a lady as you? The retort burned on Willa's tongue, but she dared not speak it. Her aunt kissed her cheek and left her at the top of the stairs to join Willa's father in the salon.

Her father's sister, born with a wild spirit, married a penniless soldier for love. Not long after their nuptials, she became a poor widow. Aunt Rosamunde never remarried, dependent upon the charity of her brother after her husband died.

Willa barely tolerated her first London Season. What a horrible occasion it had been, indeed. Girls of the *ton* twittering about, tempting eligible bachelors. Batting eyelashes with coy glances and syrupy giggles over silk fans in the name of catching a gentleman of fortune had not enticed Willa enough to play the game. Manufactured flirtations were not in Willa's armory. Why couldn't she marry for love? Why did matrimony always boil down to business?

Willa's cheeks burned at the presumption that she should be happy about this situation. She held back a retort so as not to offend her aunt. As jolly and lighthearted as Aunt Rosamunde portrayed, she was not to be trifled with when her tone proved severe. When Willa was just a girl and pressed her independent nature, her aunt had been the only adult to set her on the right path with a firm hand and frequently in a disciplinary manner to her backside.

However, Aunt Rosamunde had been less successful in preparing her niece for interactions with the opposite sex. Surely, had Willa's mother lived, she would have taught her proper etiquette, maybe even coquettish allures. Willa felt confident she would have been happily married and well on her way to having children. Her own mama had climbed from a squire's daughter to a lady without much fuss due to her charm and uncommon beauty.

She knew she should be honored that a duke would choose her as his wife. But with his recent broken betrothal, she couldn't help feeling like a desperate second choice. And she couldn't stop wondering what could have changed Lady Genevieve's mind to marry him.

How could Willa leave her home? Her papa was without a wife, having been widowed shortly after Willa's fifteenth birthday. Still, she had to admit that her father's abysmal judgment in financial matters, fueled by his excessive gaming and brandy, had earned the blame for this situation. Just another dreadful card game, and here they all were.

She licked her lips, suddenly thirsty and lightheaded. Gathering her skirts with care, Willa took a deep breath and descended the stairs. Just last week, while her father was in London gambling at White's, she had lost her footing and taken a tumble.

A footman had found her sprawled at the bottom of the staircase and summoned her maid, Edith. Willa had sworn them to secrecy. Her father's cheerful humor would be compromised should he discover his only child was so clumsy. Since Willa could stand and walk about the room with little more than a slight limp, Edith had agreed to keep the incident a secret. Willa had stayed abed for the rest of the afternoon as a precaution.

Seeing Willa in the hall, Middleton took his daughter's hands and drew her to him then kissed each cheek. "There you are, my darling Wilhemina. I hope you're ready to meet your match. He is most anxious to make your acquaintance." Her father beamed, and Willa tried to return his smile but felt the color leave her face.

If he remembers our last encounter in London, he shall likely be disappointed.

Middleton steered his daughter into the salon to meet the man himself. Willa kept her head down, studying her slippered steps peeking out from her lavender muslin gown.

Better not to make eye contact, she cautioned.

"Come, come. Let us make the introductions." Her father's voice rang with pride and satisfaction. "Here we are." He cleared his throat.

With eyes lowered, she observed the back of a well-tailored dark riding jacket, finely fitted breeches, and a pair of dusty Hessians. She wondered what sort of duke would attend a dinner party in riding boots. Wouldn't he have changed out of his riding attire for a dinner party with strangers?

"Your Grace, allow me to introduce my daughter, Miss Wilhemina Rose Middleton. Wilhemina, I present the Duke of Heighbury."

Do not look him in the eye.

He bowed, and she felt her father's feeble grip cup her shoulder. She curtsied immediately.

The duke whispered, "I hear we are to be married." He reached for her hand and lightly brushed his lips across the top. Another unwelcome spasm took over, and Willa's cheeks burned in embarrassment. She forgot herself and looked him fully in his face.

His warm brown eyes sparkled in amusement, and his firm mouth curled as if on the edge of laughter.

Perfect. Now he thinks you're trembling from his touch.

Truth be told, the duke possessed a more enticing appearance than she remembered. Dark blond waves framed his face.

He wasn't supposed to be this handsome.

Having only glimpsed his profile for a few moments in London, her imagination had conjured up a far less appealing remembrance of him.

She studied the tips of her slippers as her father chattered on about Willa's accomplishments.

She knew she was not an exquisite beauty. Willa was not ugly, but she had never turned a head strolling through Town. Reality could not change the fact that she had bloomed into merely ordinary. In a bouquet, she filled the supporting role of carnation, accentuating the beauty of other blossoms but never starring as the savored centerpiece.

With all eyes fixed on their introduction, Willa felt both an intense scrutiny and dismissal as she had the first time she had encountered the duke in London.

"And what do you enjoy, Wilhemina?"

Willa started as this stranger freely used her Christian name. The question must have had the desired shocking effect as her eyes met his playful eyes, and Willa looked away sharply.

"My niece loves to sketch. She's quite good. Perhaps you can be her next subject," Aunt Rosamunde inserted.

Willa's thoughts simmered with frustration at the suggestion. The last thing she desired was to engage her artistic abilities with this impertinent scoundrel.

"I'd very much like for you to sketch me," the duke responded, scrutinizing her entire being. "Perhaps it will help us become more intimately acquainted."

The impudence of the man. A knot rose in Willa's throat. She excused herself, pressing her forefingers to her temple.

"I believe she is a little overcome with excitement and needs a bit of fresh air," Aunt Rosamunde explained with a quick curtsy. She took Willa by the arm and led her toward French windows that opened to the terrace.

As she stepped away, Willa heard her father ask, "What do you think, Your Grace?"

"She'll do."

CHAPTER 2

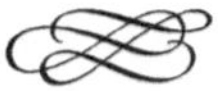

Willa spun around at the duke's words, swallowing back fiery insults ready to be unleashed. She pressed her lips together firmly, remembering her mother's words.

"A soft answer turneth away wrath: but grievous words stir up anger." Her mother often quoted from Proverbs when Willa's loose tongue had got her into trouble. She'd mostly been an agreeable child until provoked. "Hell hath no fury like a Wilhemina stirred," her family often observed. Two years without her mother's gentle admonitions had not helped her temperament.

She clutched her mother's cross, a grim reminder that her station in life remained at the sole discretion of one parent. Her father even forbade her to ride after her mother's fatal riding accident. The dutiful daughter, Willa, never once asked her father for anything of excess or to satisfy selfish desires. Her girlish wish was that she remain unmarried and by his side.

And he had bargained her to a man who simply thought she'd *do*.

Willa shouldn't feel insulted, but the duke's reply had aimed and landed solely on her pride. Frustration at the situation because of the two men coursed through her veins. The idea that she was forced to face this situation without her mother's support broke her heart. A wave of tears threatened to well within her, but outrage kept her eyes burning and dry.

"Come along now, Willa," her aunt encouraged with a tinge of urgency. "A bit of evening air will do us both good." Aunt Rosamunde also appeared to have overheard the duke's comment, but Willa was undeterred from responding.

"I beg your pardon, Your Grace?" The ice in her question could have snuffed out all the fireplaces in England.

"Oh, dear." Her father wiped his forehead with a handkerchief.

A smug grin tugged at the corner of the duke's lips. Just moments before, Willa had found him tolerable. But now, his arrogance fortified her fury.

"Have you forgotten something, Miss Middleton?" His eyes challenged her to a war of wits.

"It appears that you have forgotten your manners, Your Grace." Her response sliced through the air. Willa tilted her chin in defiance.

The room fell ominously silent.

The duke studied her expression and then beamed his approval. "Very well. I shall escort you to the terrace myself. Fresh air is wholly necessary to a sound mind *and* tongue." He offered his arm, clearly bypassing the remark aimed at his impertinence, not her need for escape.

Aunt Rosamunde fanned herself vigorously while Willa's father encouraged them. Willa's eyes pleaded with her aunt to rescue her.

The duke's agreeable response wasn't the effect Willa had hoped to achieve. She had set her bonnet for a good quarrel, forcing him to end their engagement, and he had ruined it. He wasn't playing along.

She straightened her shoulders and allowed him to escort her onto the terrace. Willa expected his touch to be cold and remote, like one of the statues in the garden. Instead, warmth from his arm added comfort and security.

Her feminine instinct to press closer to his side alarmed her. He was the enemy, not her *amour,* she reminded herself. The duke took advantage of the slight movement and placed his free hand atop hers. She stiffened in response.

When they arrived on the far side of the terrace, he dropped her arm. "My apologies, Miss Middleton. I thought it preferable to have a private conversation away from prying eyes and ears." He threw a pointed look over his shoulder at Aunt Rosamunde, who lingered near the terrace doors. "And since we're nearly married, you may call me James. James Francis Barrow, Duke of Heighbury, at your service."

"I will not impose upon your time for long, *Your Grace.*" Willa pulled her silk shawl closer around her shoulders and stepped from his reach. "My father has arranged some details which I am not privy to, apart from our bargained betrothal." She paused a moment before continuing her declaration. Reeling about to face him, she continued. "I cannot marry you."

"Cannot or will not?" The light in his chestnut eyes seemed to fade, and the smile slid from his lips. Genuine curiosity washed his expression.

Willa narrowed her eyes. The insolence of the question revealed his true character. He obviously had never been denied a whim in his entire life. And now, the only thing Willa was being denied was a life of her choosing.

"I cannot marry someone I do not like. Do not even *know*. Someone I cannot respect as you have no respect for me." She spun away from him and shivered in the cool spring air.

The duke removed his jacket and placed it on Willa's shoulders. His considerate action, accompanied by the light brush of his fingers on her skin, whirled her emotions. The heady scent of warm citrus clung to his coat, further complicating her resistance.

"I see," he finally responded after a few frosty moments of silence. "What, pray, can I do to change your opinion of me?" He turned her gently to face him.

"N-nothing," she spat. "I never asked for this betrothal. Arranged marriages are going out of fashion, in case you didn't know."

She seethed with frustration that something so barbaric had even been discussed without her permission. She continued her tirade.

"Why do you wish to marry me? You weren't even interested in dancing with me during my last Season." The fixed frown upon her countenance had likely been the culprit of her empty dance card. She met the duke's stare without remorse.

Perhaps if the duke remembered his rebuff, he would end this preposterous debacle, realizing Willa was not his match for marriage or dancing. But if that didn't work, she'd have to reveal her physical malady. When she did, her papa would most certainly be grieved.

His eyes caressed her face. He stepped to close the gap and dared to tilt her chin with his forefinger. Willa's cheeks flared as he studied her with rousing intensity.

Had he remembered her after all?

"Miss Middleton, you are not plain," he proclaimed. "You may not be a classic beauty, but you are far from unattractive."

Willa gasped. "How dare you speak to me in such a manner? When my father hears what you've said, he'll break the contract."

He laughed softly. "I highly doubt that your father will break his promise. I have it in writing, after all. Speaking of which, our bargain can only be upheld if you are amenable." The duke shrugged.

"You have what in writing? A promise to marry me off to you?"

He offered her a sly, arresting grin. "I hesitated at your father's suggestion that we marry so that you may elevate your status and secure your family's property. After thoroughly weighing the benefits, it was too good an offer to refuse." His eyes twinkled under the moonlight, challenging her convictions.

What audacity! Still, Willa struggled to keep her affections unengaged, but the warmth of his regard threatened to abduct her intentions to resist him. She stepped back, allowing the evening chill to maintain a firm wall between them.

"I am not some piece of land, sir, that you may buy and sell at will. I am the lady of this house and intend to remain here. My father will never forsake me. Not once he knows your true colors." She lifted her chin higher with each declaration.

"And I am prepared to walk away if we are not married in a fortnight per the contract. Should the wedding not occur, your father will lose the entire estate as recompense for his gaming debt. Those are the terms. And you and your father will be left destitute in time." He crossed his arms.

Willa removed his jacket and shoved it at him. "I have never in my life met such an arrogant and soulless creature. You are without salvation of any kind."

She bobbed a quick curtsy and strode toward Aunt Rosamunde, whose eyes widened at the scene. "I am feeling poorly, Aunt. I would like to lie down."

"Good night, *Willa*," he called out. The arrogance of

gaining the last word using her familiar name sent a searing heat through her bones. Whether the sensation permeated from righteous anger or involuntary attraction, she could not say.

Willa bolted toward the French windows and meant to toss the duke an icy look to demonstrate her displeasure. Instead, she observed him draw her shawl to his nose, his mouth twitching in amusement.

Her shawl! It was wrapped up in his jacket.

He captured her eyes with his and winked, forcing her mouth open in astonishment. She stomped toward her shocked aunt, yielding her favorite silk to the duke.

CHAPTER 3

Charlie, the Irish undergroom of Middleton Grange, handed James the reins. He pulled himself into the saddle in one swift motion.

"Good morning, Your Grace."

"How do you find your young mistress, Miss Middleton?" he inquired of the young man.

The undergroom tugged on his hat. "Now, I shouldn't speak outta turn, but Miss Middleton is a bucket of sunshine so long as ye don't threaten her with rain."

James snorted. "So I gathered." Since their introduction, her trying nature sent him entirely out of kilter.

"Pardon me, Your Grace, for sayin' so, but the young miss really is a good girl. Been through a lot losin' her mam so young is all. And with her papa down and out over it, she's had a mite unfair load pressed on her shoulders." Charlie offered a quick bow, then sauntered back toward the stables.

James considered the undergroom's words as he stroked the horse's head. He knew nothing of Willa but needed to find a way to win the battle brought on by a ridiculous wager that would save them both.

So long as he married by the time he reached his thirtieth birthday next month, Heighbury Manor and the fortune he inherited would remain his. Otherwise, his entire heritage would be passed to a cousin in Wales. Only an empty title of duke would remain.

Willa exhibited the epitome of a respectable lady, serene though ordinary. Once he'd stirred the fire in her hazel eyes, he wanted to keep it stoked and burning. To his astonishment, she'd challenged him and unabashedly so.

He hadn't expected the spirited exchange. No woman had ever turned down an opportunity to be seen on his arm. He'd had more than one eager mama encourage a marriage proposal. It was preposterous. In fact, he was considered quite the catch among the *ton* and had broken many female hearts. James could have bedded them all if he hadn't been raised with proper morals.

"A colossal failure," he muttered, taking off at rapid speed. Middleton had promised him that his daughter would be thrilled for the match. The man had promised that what his daughter lacked in refined beauty, she more than made up for in intelligence and loyalty.

Loyalty was what he needed. He had been betrayed by more than one friend, especially in business matters. Sir Lawrence D'Arby, the man responsible for this predicament, topped that list. This would be the last gaming scheme he'd make if he couldn't secure the marriage.

He'd been surprised at Middleton's offer of his daughter's hand when he'd saved the old baronet from the conniving, traitorous D'Arby since their boyhood days at Eton. Even though James intervened with a plan of his own, Middleton's tongue was set to wag with each pour of brandy, offering up his flesh and blood to save his hide.

At first, he had been amused by the man's ramblings. As he considered the acquisition of Middleton's estate while sitting across from D'Arby, an idea took on a life of its own. Acquiring more land provided the perfect solution to his compulsive need to win and his necessity to wed.

He'd been reminded many times that he needed a wife. Time was slipping away with his birthday on the horizon. He had initially scoffed at the man's offer of his daughter's hand. As Middleton described his daughter with endearment, his interest was piqued. Love needn't be part of the equation.

He had never been in love, although one lady in particular, Lady Genevieve, would have become the Duchess of Heighbury had she not betrayed him with D'Arby.

For the hundredth time, at least since this agreement came about, James mulled over the serendipity of the situation. What a satisfying, proper payback to D'Arby and his former betrothed. Their betrayal wounded his pride and trust, costing him his reputation with the London gossips.

Although he'd become an increasingly popular figure to scoff and revere, none of it mattered to him. He allowed his reputation and that of his family to be darkened so that he could escape the match. He preferred taking his chances with his fortune by not securing a marriage to being cuckolded in society by an openly unfaithful spouse.

And then he remembered Willa from that very London ball.

Two of his acquaintances had attempted to steer him to dance with her in a ballroom full of young ladies preening and prowling for a future husband. On the contrary, she remained at the perimeter, quietly observing the event and with apparent indifference.

He had considered caving to the dare by two earls in asking her to dance, but he remembered Genevieve and thought better than to give the young miss consequence after being slighted by others. Whilst more than a handful of young ladies had shown obvious interest in him, he merely nodded and left to find his betrothed.

Quitting the ballroom in search of her, sounds from a secluded corner had drawn him into the scene. Genevieve and D'Arby. In a most compromising embrace. James's gaze locked with hers, hauteur and ecstasy filling her face.

He wasn't as angry at the betrayal as he should have been. Panic surged in his chest when he realized his fortune was in jeopardy. Without a wife, he would not inherit what was rightfully his, per his father's will.

The memory of Willa on that London night contrasted with their meeting at Middleton Grange. Hope of finding a trustworthy marriage partner had eluded him since his broken engagement last year. Providence had cracked the door open for a sliver of light to burst into the dark corners of despair and rescue him from misfortune.

He choked back aggravation at Willa's admission of why she would not want to marry him. As his mind replayed the scene over, her person grew in appeal. She was not ill-favored. At first glance, she wouldn't bring a man to his knee with a marriage proposal with her cool exterior, yet, given the chance, she might unlock his heart despite her impervious demeanor.

With unexpected skill, her impassioned response had invited him in for a closer look. Perhaps she was not the unassuming wallflower he'd glimpsed at the ball in London. But what he observed within the depths of her impenetrable façade irked him. She'd stormed off in an unladylike huff, leaving him holding her shawl and wondering what the deuce had happened.

When she'd turned, no doubt to rebuke him again, her eyes studied him long enough to tempt him to raise her shawl to his lips. He stared back, waiting in silence. If her aunt hadn't pulled her away, he might have teased her a bit more. Instead, contempt shone in her scrutiny, and the women hurried inside.

He neared the edge of the parcel included in the agreement and reined in the horse. A fetching property unfolded before him with large, rolling hills and a landscape dotted with wildflowers.

He reached into his coat pocket, drew her shawl to his nose, and inhaled the subtle scent of lilacs clinging to the silk. Did she really detest him, or was she merely making a poor attempt at playacting? The challenge was on, and he refused to lose the lady's hand.

James grimaced as he prompted the horse forward. The more his mind attempted to push away the disgust in Willa's eyes, the harder he pushed the creature beneath him.

* * *

"WILLA, my girl. Won't you please meet with the duke? I'm assured he bears no ill will toward you even though you behaved most childishly last night." Her father pleaded as he neared her bedside. "I do hope the duke was not too uncomfortable with your demonstration."

Aunt Rosamunde chimed. "Dearest, you are fortunate that the man wants to marry you yet."

Willa sank under the blankets, pulling them over her head. *This is my bed, and I will not be torn from it.*

"Go away," she moaned in protest. All she wanted was her mother's soothing voice and patient reassurance. Warm memories of her mother were pleasant and wrapped in love. She had understood Willa as her father had not. Both mother and daughter had been born with similar headstrong and fierce personalities.

"Please be reasonable, Daughter. I insist. You have been in

bed most of the day. The man will find you lazy and difficult." He patted the covers more firmly than the first time.

Willa tossed the blankets, revealing her disheveled hair tumbling loose from a braid.

"I am not a business transaction, Papa."

Middleton sighed. "My dear, this is how things are. You are at an age where you must marry. I will not peacefully join your mother in the next life until I am certain that your place in this life is decided. He is a duke, after all, and can provide you a home and comforts beyond your imagination." He crossed his arms over his chest. "Please, child. The papers are signed. Would you prefer that I die a ruined gentleman?"

"Oh, Brother, you are not at death's door," Aunt Rosamunde responded with an eye roll. "Your papa is correct, however," she scolded Willa. "One day, your father will depart from this earth. Make us all happy, dear girl, and settle the bargain without delay."

Willa stared blankly at the ceiling, feeling betrayed by her aunt for conspiring against her. She had not considered why her father would want her married, only that it had been arranged from his brandy-infused actions and without her approval.

"But he does not love me. I'm merely part of a contract," she countered.

Her father chuckled softly. "Oh, my dear. Most marriages are borne out of duty and respect, not love. It's the greatest responsibility one can bear."

Willa craned her neck to search his face. "Didn't you love Mama?"

Her father took her hand in his. "Most decidedly. But not at first. She was, of course, beautiful, but her headstrong nature and sharp tongue could be off-putting. Much like yours." He smiled. "Our love grew over time and even more so with you." He tapped a forefinger on the tip of her nose to punctuate his confession.

"I do not even like him, Papa. And I promise you I cannot grow to love a man who would threaten to leave us penniless if I do not do as he says." She gestured to her aunt. "That isn't love of any sort." She sniffed, her countenance unchanged.

"I fear I have allowed you far too much independence. Ever since your mama left us, I wanted to ensure that your life would be one of comfort and ease, even if it meant you managed your own temperament. To my utter disappointment, you fail to behave reasonably."

"Papa, you must find another way to relieve your debt. Perhaps your friend, Sir Wayfield, can lend you the sum. But, please. You can't make me marry him."

Her father surrendered with a sigh and left the room. She watched him retreat, his back hunched in defeat.

And you fail to recognize the countless occasions after drowning your sorrows in brandy when I acted as your nursemaid.

Willa twisted the coverlet in her hands. "You know the duke's reputation, Aunt. He cannot mean to love me while pursuing other ladies. Why else would Lady Genevieve have ended their betrothal in scandal if he were not undesirable as a husband?"

Aunt Rosamunde threw back the blankets, eliciting a cry from her niece. "Alright, Wilhemina. You have had your scene. It is time to abandon your childish ways and conduct yourself as a proper young lady. Mind, do not listen to the gossipy, jealous young ladies in ballrooms. You will dress and come down to meet with your betrothed."

"I have not consented to be his wife, Aunt!"

"But your father has. Half an hour. I'll give you half an hour, or I will come up here and fetch you myself. Are we in agreement?"

Willa knew better than to object to her aunt when her tone threw darts and ultimatums.

"Yes, Aunt."

"Good. And mind that he is a *duke*. You are to be a *duchess*. Conduct yourself in a manner worthy of the man. You shan't find one on every corner in Town." Aunt Rosamunde looked over her shoulder once more on her way out the door. "Half an hour," she repeated sternly.

Thirty-one minutes later, Willa joined the Duke of Heighbury with her family in the library.

For a moment, she expected the devilish grin she'd provoked the night before from him but was met with a scowl instead.

"There now. She's here, Your Grace."

Willa searched the duke's face for a hint of joy, even humor, to see her but found none. A slight twinge of longing surprised her.

"I apologize for my tardiness, Your Grace." She bobbed a quick curtsy, which drew a curt nod from the duke. Her eyes froze on his lips for a moment before she looked away.

"Say, it's a lovely day for a walk. The sun is quite brilliant. Willa, why don't you and the duke enjoy a stroll in the gardens?" Aunt Rosamunde's ringlets bounced in agreement with her own suggestion.

Willa's chest tightened. *What a sad pair we must make. Neither of us can tolerate the other.*

"But tea will be served shortly," Willa offered, her voice low and smooth.

"You have plenty of time." Aunt Rosamunde escorted them to the door.

Reluctantly, Willa retrieved her bonnet from her maid and followed James outside.

They wandered down the garden path in silence, side by

side. When they reached a small pond, his voice broke their silence with an awkward huskiness.

"Tell me about the garden here."

Willa cut her eyes to him. "It was my mother's garden. It has flowers and shrubs. Just like any other, I suppose."

He laughed, the twinkle returning to his eyes. "That is much like saying a rose is just a rose."

"Are you fond of Shakespeare, Your Grace?" She lowered herself on a nearby bench.

"I appreciate a good sonnet or two." He grinned, then gestured to sit down. Willa acquiesced, allowing him room. "I possess many other qualities aside from proper education and etiquette. In fact, there's quite a lot you don't know about me, *Wilhemina Rose Middleton*." His tight expression relaxed as he accented her full Christian name.

To her dismay, she engaged the conversation with ease. "I am eager to learn."

He removed his hat and then twirled it between his hands. "This is quite the change of heart from last night when you shoved my jacket and your shawl at me."

She eyed him with a calculated expression. "I do not wish for my behavior of last night to reflect poorly on my family. Such shocking revelations of your arrangement with my father cannot be expected to be embraced with open arms."

"I am truly remorseful if my sudden appearance affected you so profoundly. I desire that we enter our acquaintance on *affectionate* terms."

Willa had not expected a genteel response to her attempt at an apology. Her mind reeled with a new tactic. Perhaps if she appeared congenial rather than aloof, she could persuade him that marrying her was the last thing that would bring either of them happiness. His former rebuff in London had been proof of that much. She would find another way to save the estate.

"What do you suggest?"

"To begin, you may call me James, and I would like to address you as Willa." He raised her gloved hand to his mouth, lowering his lips to brush the top of her gloved knuckles.

"Perhaps." She withdrew her hand from his, her fingers beginning to tremble. Despite his flirtatious gesture, she determined to steer their conversation toward the marriage contract. "You wore military riding boots last night. My father was a brave soldier long ago."

"Ah. I'm delighted to hear that you admire something about me." He grinned. "In fact, I had decided to become familiar with the property before the dinner party. I rode out onto the estate and lost track of the time. And when I came into the house, I realized my error but was far too impatient for our introduction to change." He leaned in, forcing her eyes to meet his. "Thank the good Lord, my valet reminded me this morning that I must *at least* wear suitable footwear tonight to avoid offending you further. He is responsible and extremely *loyal*."

Warm shades of pink reached Willa's cheeks. "A f-fine trait, indeed." She grasped at her throat, wholly unnerved at his proximity.

"Perhaps you could enlighten me about your life here at Middleton Grange." He shifted away and crossed his arms in polite decorum.

"What do you wish to know?"

"Everything." The duke's brown eyes softened.

Willa looked away quickly. Was he baiting her? Testing her? Surely, her father had described their home.

"You've seen most everything there is to see, surely. We are blessed with more than we need." She swept her arm toward the house. "I certainly do not require a larger dwelling than this." She stole a sideways look, waiting for his response.

"It is a lovely estate, to be sure. I am surprised to hear that you do not entertain often."

"My father stopped hosting parties after my mother died. She loved entertaining visitors in our home." Willa twisted her lips in thought. Middleton Grange was a grandiose home with plenty of space for parties. "My favorite childhood memories include hiding behind the ballroom doors to spy on the festivities. Guests laughed and danced until the early morning hours, permeating the halls with joy and vibrancy. Watching my mother dress in her finest gowns for the occasions filled me with longing for the day when I would have my first Season."

When it came and passed without her mother's guiding hand, Willa's eyes had been opened to the business of relationships devoid of romance. She regretted taking part in the superficial custom even more so when not one man had asked her to join him in a quadrille.

"You should smile more, dearest," Aunt Rosamunde had advised at parties when she'd been left *sans* a dancing partner. "Tea tastes better with a bit of honey, you know."

A slight breeze passed through the garden, inducing a chill. Willa rubbed her shoulders. The duke reached into his coat pocket. "Before I forget, you left this in my jacket last night." He withdrew the shawl she had worn, neatly folded. As she reached out to accept it, her right hand quivered so intensely that she wrapped her left hand over it and settled both hands in her lap. The trembling did not pass unnoticed. His eyes widened with curiosity, and his lips curved into a worried frown.

"Allow me." He wrapped it around her shoulders, tying the ends into a loose knot.

He sat forward and looked at her intently. She allowed

her eyes to settle into his, unable to move or think. If he moved any closer, their noses would touch.

"How long have you had the tremor?" he finally asked.

"What can you mean? I'm just a little hungry. I haven't eaten today." Willa dipped her chin, unwilling to meet his searching gaze. At least he hadn't been rude. She expected him to goad her into a verbal spar.

"Let us remedy that then, shall we? Tea should be ready." He helped her gain her feet, forcing her to look at him. His hold lingered, an invitation waiting in the depths of his eyes.

Taking an unsteady breath, Willa accepted the duke's arm, and they returned to the house in silence. Again.

CHAPTER 4

A pang of sympathy ran through James when he and Willa joined her father and aunt for tea. He pondered how fearful it must be to be told that your family's future depended on leaving home to marry a stranger. He hadn't considered how their predicament might affect her until their congenial, rather pleasant exchange in the garden.

Although hesitant to converse with her so soon after their thorny introduction, Middleton had convinced James to meet with his daughter earlier that morning. "Talk to her and assure her, Your Grace. If you knew her, you would see she is most like her mother and craves calm and consistency, even if you cannot detect it in her mien."

James was out of his depth. Usually, his charm and title were enough. Willa's initial reaction in fleeing from his presence had sent him askew.

When she finally appeared wearing a pastel blue gown that accented the red shimmer in her hair, he felt shame and remorse for his gauche behavior and repudiation at the London ball. He had hardly given it a thought then, so absorbed in his own conflict, too distracted with Genevieve's absence.

Willa was not just pleasantly appealing. Her beauty was unique and fragile. Sunlight met her hazel eyes and reflected radiant beams, warm and composed.

The realization hit him in his chest that he had not wanted her to be alluring. It would have been easier if she had been plain. The more beautiful a wife, the easier other men seduced them.

Just like Genevieve.

Willa's enchantment ignited from the embers behind her eyes and cascaded down her cheeks, landing on a faintly rosy mouth. James understood at once that her delicate mouth could either cut a man's pride in half or kiss away his uncertainty.

After they sat by the fish pond, he'd noticed that she trembled when he handed her the forgotten shawl. Realization dawned on him. She hadn't shaken with excitement at their meeting. Something was amiss, and he determined to uncover the source.

When their lips had nearly touched, he'd fought every instinct to crush his mouth to hers and bury his face in an enticing scent of lilacs that lingered at her throat. Given the proper encouragement, he could make a lady's toes curl in her slippers from a simple embrace.

"How marvelous. I see you two are properly making your acquaintance." James dropped Willa's arm as Willa's aunt, Mrs. Livingston, clapped her hands together in satisfaction.

The only means to satisfy him would be if he could take another turn with Willa, allowing her inner sunlight to embrace them with affection. Given just a little more time, he was sure he could seduce her emotions.

Alas, time was not their friend. The covenant needed to be completed within a fortnight, or else D'Arby would return to collect the debt James had promised yet not paid on behalf of Willa's father. His finances were already in jeopardy should he not marry by his next birthday. James suspected that was why D'Arby seduced Genevieve away from him and attempted to woo her into a marriage benefiting his bank account with James's inheritance. The rogue was not above deception or blackmail to prove his reputation.

James forced his mind to the conversation in the room. Middleton rambled on about their London meeting before heralding his daughter's accomplishments. Mrs. Livingston swiftly reminded him of her artistic abilities, too.

He drank in the layers of red and brown in her curls as he followed her to the divan. "Would you sketch me, Willa?" he whispered into her hair as they sat down. James intended to discover every talent she possessed. He would use whatever tools of flattery he possessed to persuade her into marriage.

A slight frown appeared at the edges of her mouth.

"If you would like," she responded.

"Perfect. After supper, I would be most obliged." He sipped his tea and placed his hand on his thigh. Just a few inches to the right, and he would be touching her hand. Absently, he allowed his pinky finger to brush her wrist lightly.

He detected a hitch in her breathing but remained silent. Catching the slight change in her complexion, he vowed that by the morning of their wedding, he would stir her desire to be his wife.

* * *

WILLA'S BODY TREMBLED, but not from the tremors that had been plaguing her. Warmth filled her senses when he neared.

This would not do. First, she resented him. Then she feared him. Now she *liked* him.

Her heart should know better. Before breakfast, she'd overheard Cook whispering to Edith, revealing a list of ladies he'd been connected to in London. Despite his reputation with romancing ladies of the *ton* and a scandalous broken engagement to the daughter of a marquess, she imagined herself desired by a man of prominence.

In her daydreams, she teetered on the brink of escaping to London and forging a new life or surrendering to the rules of society for all women. It didn't help matters that the duke had shown kindness to her even as she swore to loathe him on principle alone.

A moment of understanding and compassion was exchanged between them in the garden after he'd seen her shaking hand but hadn't run away. He'd even inquired about the tremor with vexing concern.

At his insistence, they had retired to the drawing room after supper with her father and aunt, who perched on the settee. Aunt Rosamunde busied herself with needlework while Middleton read aloud from Proverbs.

James's eyes fixed out the window over her shoulder while she outlined his face.

She'd loved drawing since she was a young girl. It was her favorite entertainment for guests. She was quick with brief sketches, mainly consisting of her father's business associates and their wives.

As James faced her, she allowed her eyes to drink him in. He was undeniably handsome, humor playing about his kindly mouth. A lock of hair drooped down the middle of his forehead. Of course, she knew of his skill at wooing ladies. But, she resolved not to become one of his conquests.

"Have you finished?" he asked, not for the first time.

Willa pressed her lips together to keep from smiling. The man couldn't sit for more than two minutes before feeling compelled to speak.

"No. Please be still." The pencil slid across the paper as swiftly as she dared. The likeness must be perfect. With the shadows from the darkened room illuminated by only a few candles, Willa feared she wouldn't catch him in quite the right light. Perhaps she should suggest they start again tomorrow morning after breakfast.

"You're quite bewitching when you're concentrating," he added after another two minutes. "Your eyes flicker in the candlelight, and you bite your lip as if tasting a strawberry."

Willa's cheeks heated. No matter their presumed betrothal, his notions were indeed scandalous. Her eyes darted toward Aunt Rosamunde and Papa, praying they hadn't heard him trying to make love to her.

"And you are quite annoying. How ever am I to finish if you don't keep quiet?"

And you're annoyingly charming, she wanted to add but held her tongue instead.

He dipped his head in mock shame. "You promised to call me James. And I apologize. Please continue. I promise not to open my mouth again until the artist permits me."

Willa longed to reach out and touch his arm in reassurance but was determined to finish the sketch. Within the hour, she had studied every inch of his striking face. He was not ruggedly handsome, but his countenance was friendly and inviting. His eyes, like chocolate, glowed in the dim lighting. The bridge above his slightly crooked nose pinched in concentration. But his full lips invited her to join his good humor.

She kept her free hand firmly in her lap so as not to caress his cheek with familiar affection. No wonder the ladies were drawn to his affable demeanor.

"I do not possess an array of social graces with strangers. It is easier for me to draw them in silence than speak with them." Willa swallowed as she dared to look him full in the face.

"How do you expect to sketch them well if you don't engage in conversation?" he whispered. The sincerity of his question hammered at her heart.

Who was the subject now?

The warmth in his voice invited her in for a closer examination. When he turned toward her, a sudden tremor caused her to drop the pencil. The instinct to flatten her palm and catch it forced a large mark across the sketch.

"Oh, no. I've ruined it."

James reached out, taking her shaking hand in his. Their eyes met, and an intimacy she had not experienced enveloped her.

"May I see?" he asked in a hushed tone.

Willa extended the likeness to him. She eyed him in expectation, awaiting his verdict. His expression stilled.

A few moments later, a grin overtook his features. "You are truly talented. It's lovely."

"Except for that graphite mark across your face," Willa added with a frown.

"A slight improvement, wouldn't you say?" His laughing eyes brightened in the dim glow of the room.

Willa's mouth twitched with delight. This couldn't be the man she vowed to despise that very morning. This man teased her and laughed at his own expense. She longed to join his amusement, but reality contrasted with her desires as she remembered why he was here. Fear bubbled up inside her again, knowing she was being sold off with a piece of property and not truly desired for love.

Foolish girl, he's playing you like a fiddle. You are nothing more than a financial arrangement to him.

Her thoughts reeling, she withdrew her hand.

"It is yours to keep then. Perhaps it is an improvement. I daresay it is more a revelation of your character." She stood abruptly.

James's brow furrowed, and the gleam in his eyes extinguished from her attack. "You are correct. I am faulty to an extreme. All sinners are." He stood and towered over her. "And yet by grace, I am forgiven my follies. Good night, Miss Middleton." He dipped his head and exited.

"Good heavens, what have you done to the duke now?" Aunt Rosamunde crossed the room anxiously. Willa's father looked up from his Bible with a quizzical brow.

"Nothing, Aunt. And I never shall. I bid you both goodnight." She dropped the sketchbook on the chair before retiring to bed.

Willa's heart weighed heavy as she trudged up the steps to her bedroom. It was easier to guard her heart with a stone wall than open herself to the unknown, where she had no control.

* * *

RECLINING IN A CHAIR by the fire, James stared into the flames and watched them flicker. He'd considered packing his bag and leaving before morning. Blast! He'd tried to do himself and the baronet a favor by marrying his daughter. She was not only reluctant but positively resistant to becoming his wife.

Granted, he had flirted audaciously with her as she sketched him and probably deserved a good wigging. James couldn't help himself. Her delicate and ethereal appearance was magnified in the candlelight as she focused on him. Alluring dimples appeared each time she pressed her lips together in concentration. Her artistic skill unnerved him. Any other woman he fancied would be sure to catch his best features. Willa had captured every imperfect line in his countenance and unruly hair.

The floral fragrance of her skin intoxicated him to the point where he'd become undone. He would have dared to dot kisses along her jawline had Middleton and Mrs. Livingston not been present. James was well-versed in the art of stealing kisses and women's hearts. But Willa's heart exhibited an unwillingness to be conquered.

And then there were her tremors.

James bit his lip as he remembered that Willa's hand shook almost violently for a second time in his presence. Middleton had never mentioned any illness. After getting to know her in just two days, he could only assume she hadn't disclosed the condition to anyone.

Perhaps he should consult with his family physician. He sent up a silent prayer that it was nothing more than a good dose of nerves—he knew he sometimes had an aphrodisiacal effect on women.

Lud, what difference would it make if she continued to combat his attempts to secure the marriage?

James paced the room, debating if even the land would be worth the trouble. He didn't need it to expand his fortune; he only needed to gain a wife to secure it. When he married and produced an heir, his bloodline would continue and be settled for generations to come.

The situation proved difficult. James wanted to help Middleton, but at what cost to himself? Time spent attempting to win Willa's heart could be better spent with less challenging prospects. A quick laugh erupted when he considered how similar he and Willa were in their lack of conversational decorum. He'd always skirted along the fence of society's standards. She seemed to dismiss them altogether.

Yet the common goal of carving their own path would either be an obstacle or an opportunity.

Stay the course. After all, James wasn't keen on failing at love or money.

CHAPTER 5

A slight drizzle didn't deter Willa from walking the garden the morning after her botched attempt to sketch the duke. She shook the thought away, reveling in her momentary escape from him, Papa, and Aunt Rosamunde. In fact, she welcomed the raindrops kissing her cheeks. When she was a little girl, her mother would take her by the hand and run outside during rainstorms. They skipped through puddles until her father chastised them for tempting an illness and muddying their hems.

So much had changed since her mother's death, but the familiar sensations bestowed glad memories. Earthy fragrance mixed in the air with refreshing rain impressed on her heart that her mother wasn't so far away.

As she circled the house, she wondered if her mother would approve of James. Considering what her mother would have felt about the arrangement, Willa knew she would never have been sold to the highest bidder.

A shadowy figure approaching recaptured her thoughts. Pulling his hat lower to dispel some of the water collected on the brim, a gallant (or annoyed, she couldn't quite tell) duke sprinted toward her and removed his cloak. He held it over her head as he coaxed her inside.

"Why should you care whether or not I catch a cold?" Willa dared.

"In spite of our circumstances, I do not wish to be thought a cad and leave you to fall ill before we are to be married. I saw you walking the gardens just now without so much as a bonnet to cover your head." He removed her cloak once they arrived at the door and gently dabbed at her wet face with a handkerchief.

"You presume, Your Grace, I have acquiesced to marrying you. Further, a little spring shower never hurt anyone." Willa tipped her face to the sky. "If the flowers can manage it, so can I. In case you weren't aware, I am far less delicate." She jutted her chin, eliciting a chuckle from the duke.

"Not to worry, Miss Middleton. Next time you decide to wander in the rain, I will leave you to it, whatever the consequences may be." He offered an exaggerated bow and disappeared inside.

* * *

An hour after his feeble attempt at a polite exchange with Willa, James's valet Barnaby, assisted him with his overcoat and escorted him to his carriage.

"I won't be gone too long. However, if I return late, assure Middleton and Miss Middleton are informed not to wait. They are to dine with or without me."

Barnaby nodded.

James chewed the inside of his lip, a nasty habit his

governess had tried to break him of but failed. He'd risen that morning, resolved to quit the entire situation and allow D'Arby to collect Middleton's debt by whatever means he deemed necessary. James had tried to help Sir Edgar—and himself—but all his efforts had produced nothing.

I should wash my hands of this predicament.

He'd received a message from D'Arby and agreed to meet him at a coaching inn halfway between Hampshire and London. He knew what the cad wanted. An update, no doubt, on where all stood on the disastrous agreement. Sleep had eluded him as he'd toyed with the notion of canceling the contract. Regret at inserting himself into Middleton's drunken folly churned his stomach. He closed his eyes for the remainder of the journey in a feeble attempt to settle his mind. Instead, a sweet pout beneath sparkling hazel eyes diverted his thoughts.

Well into the afternoon, he arrived and was immediately met with a grin on D'Arby's smug face.

"I was beginning to think you'd changed your mind." He slapped James on the back.

"I had a late start."

The men entered the inn and sat at a table close to the fire. D'Arby ordered an ale while James chose tea. Alcohol produced this situation; the less he drank, the better.

D'Arby leaned forward. "So. How are Middleton and your betrothed?" he asked with a lick of the lips.

If James had not been raised in the church and taught to follow the Ten Commandments, he would have struck D'Arby across the face–or worse. Instead, he swallowed back a bold response and allowed his eyes to observe everyone in the inn save for his foe.

"They appear to be well."

"I see." He clasped his hands around the mug on the table.

"With that matter settled, let's discuss our business agreement, shall we? I assume you recall what is at stake here."

With a brief nod, James sipped his tea.

"And you are certain the terms shall be fulfilled in due time?"

James cut his eyes to D'Arby. "As you say. In due time."

"Your birthday draws closer, as well as the due date for your payment to me. Nevertheless, if your current *slip of muslin* cannot bring herself to accept your proposal, I could help you find a suitable replacement."

James jumped to his feet from the insult aimed at Willa, rattling his teacup and sending D'Arby's ale on its side. The contents slid across the table and dripped onto the floor.

The men stared at each other briefly before D'Arby rose and extended a hand. James stood and crossed his arms over his chest. D'Arby laughed.

"You always were a stubborn lot, *Your Grace*. It keeps our relationship quite lively."

Lively was not the word James would use to describe their family ties.

"Have you taken on more than you can wager, Cousin?" D'Arby continued.

The question intended to provoke James yet aroused more conflicting feelings within his spirit. Friends, they were not. Regardless, he offered a tight smile. Yearning for the end of his dealings with D'Arby fueled his renewed determination to secure Willa's hand as swiftly as possible.

* * *

SUPPER THAT EVENING was a rather subdued affair. Willa and James kept their communication to superficial pleasantries. Willa's father and Aunt Rosamunde attempted to include the two in conversation, but neither took the hint. The silver clinked against the porcelain dinner plates, contributing to the cheerless atmosphere.

As the four retired to the drawing room, Aunt Rosamunde approached Willa.

"Dear, why not sketch the duke again? If you weren't satisfied with your first attempt, I'm sure he would appreciate another try. Hmm?" Aunt Rosamunde nodded, but Willa frowned at the suggestion.

"I don't think so, Aunt. He endured quite enough of my worst rendering." She preferred to exhibit and began playing scales, looking up every few moments to glimpse James's reaction.

His brows rose as she transitioned seamlessly to a staccato tune. Aunt Rosamunde hummed along and smiled at the duke.

"She's quite the talent, is she not, Your Grace?" Aunt Rosamunde offered.

"Indeed. I'm impressed." He joined Willa at the pianoforte to turn the pages for her. Her insides warmed from his nearness, causing her to miss a note. She willed herself to concentrate, her lips pulling into a tight line.

He leaned forward slightly, and the spicy scent clinging to his sleeve blurred her senses. Her foot slipped from the pedal, creating an awkward clang. She pulled her hands from the keys and pressed them into her lap.

"That's enough for tonight."

James cupped her shoulder with his hand. She froze from his touch, her mind and body shuddering from the heat of his skin.

"Willa, please continue. You play so well." He ran his thumb lightly across her shoulder.

Preposterous flirt.

Resisting the urge to swat his hand away, she closed her eyes and willed her emotions into control. Desiring him to leave her presence fought against the longing for him to pull her into the comfort of his arms. Her emotions scaled up and down like the keys beneath her. If only she'd paid attention to her Season in London, perhaps she would have a better command of conversing with gentlemen.

His magnetism both irritated her and forced unwanted thoughts of tucking herself in the crook of his arm and settling into his side. She knew well enough not to succumb to such impulse in the presence of her family or face certain reproach. Besides, she'd vowed to despise him and would not deign to marry such an outrageously egotistical rascal.

He would never catch her heart if she could conquer her feelings. His romantic overtures no longer vexed her to an indignant reply. A soft sigh escaped her lips in resignation. Gesturing to the bench, she moved over so he could sit down.

"I'm not a horrible monster, ravenous to eat you alive, you know." James eased beside her with a grin, sending her heart into skips and leaps.

"You cannot understand me. How is that the basis for a good marriage?" Willa toyed with the lace on her gown.

He shifted his body toward her, allowing his forearm to settle above the keys. "I would like to understand you very much. It may take a lifetime, but what an adventure that might be." Lifting her bare fingertips, he raised them to his lips, then lightly replaced her hand to her side before Aunt Rosamunde or her father could catch the intimate gesture.

Their eyes locked, and for several seconds, neither spoke. James lifted the music sheet and shielded their faces from her family.

"By the by, you are quite the vision this evening," he whispered, his eyes roaming her face.

For a brief moment, Willa's resolve faded. Her lips parted,

daring him to attempt a kiss. To her disappointment, he merely smiled and then lowered the sheet.

"Goodnight, Miss Middleton."

However, pressing her mouth to his eager lips was an impossible notion, so Willa remained frozen on the bench as he retired for the night. Her breath heavy and flustered, he'd outwitted her once again with the last word.

CHAPTER 6

James's confidence was reflected in his stride for the first time since his arrival at Middleton Grange. He headed to the stables for a midnight ride and to consider his situation. Taking his horse out into the night, he found a spot under an old oak to ponder the contract with Middleton. And to relive the moment when he'd nearly kissed her.

At the piano, he'd glimpsed hope in Willa's eyes when he knew he could have brushed his lips against hers, knowing she would have welcomed his kiss.

And yet it frightened him.

For the briefest moments, he had considered confessing his motives behind wanting to marry her. He'd wanted to take her in his arms and assure her that the stipulation of keeping his estate no longer mattered to him. His heart had opened to receive her not just for business but for love.

In that same flash of thought, he'd seen the disgust return in the green flecks of her eyes. So he bid her goodnight and retired to pace a hole in the rug of his bedchamber to consider other alternatives. When that didn't produce the desired clarity, he'd decided to go for a moonlit ride.

Perhaps he would do better to revise the terms, releasing Willa to the freedom she so obviously desired. That would leave him purchasing only a parcel of land and no hope of acquiring the rest upon Middleton's death. They weren't happy thoughts, but the reality of societal traditions rarely elicited joyous circumstances.

He turned the horse around and studied the outline of Middleton Grange in the silvery moonlight. Would Willa be sleeping soundly, or was she awake with similar musings? His eyes scanned the windows, wondering which one was hers.

Despite his logical leanings, he wanted to protect Willa from the apparent outcome should she never marry. He'd also grown fond of the household staff who would be forced to find new employment. Charlie, the undergroom, had proved invaluable in preparing his horses. He toyed with bringing him on at Heighbury Manor with a promotion if he could convince Middleton.

The family would be destitute should they continue down the path with the current contract and D'Arby's interference. Without the wedding, Willa had no other recourse and no family to account for except her cousin, Miss Cassandra Lawton.

He learned Willa's mother's niece had been orphaned as an infant. Cassandra's father had relations in London who had taken her in as their own. Mr. Buntling, a vicar, and his wife reared her until she was of age. Then Cassandra assumed a position in the Cronwell home as Lady Cronwell's companion. Lord Cronwell, a distinct member of Parliament, and his wife attended Mr. Buntling's services religiously. Since she was further down on the rung of society than

Willa, the only way out was for one of the Middleton ladies to marry.

He doubted Mrs. Livingston sought to remarry. Willa's aunt appeared to lead a satisfactory life as a soldier's widow, relying solely on her brother's charity. Middleton would undoubtedly find himself in a pickle without a roof over his head or access to the brandy that induced him to reckless behavior.

"Confound it all," he muttered. D'Arby was the true scoundrel behind all this complicated nonsense. Should Willa agree to the nuptials, he would only purchase one parcel of land, leaving Middleton with most of his property and income intact.

Should she refuse him, he'd take all of Middleton Grange and likely sell it off to recoup some of his fortune. Wretched D'Arby had forced his hand that fateful evening to rescue a drunken soul with no hope against a conniving criminal.

"Ridiculous circumstances," he grumbled.

James reached into his jacket and retrieved the folded sketch he'd pocketed as he left the bedchamber. Willa was a true talent with just a pencil, capturing him more astutely than the watercolor portrait in his study. The morning after the botched sketch, he had risen early and found it on the chair she had perched the evening before. He slipped it into his jacket, keeping it close to his heart.

What a fool he was for thinking her feelings were warming toward him. She'd examined every flaw in his face and found him unacceptable. But her hand had drawn him remarkably well. She had revealed a life that encompassed an eventful history and the truth in the mischief behind his eyes that he had lived like a fool in his youth, down to the hint of laughter that twitched one side of his lips.

He had gambled his fortune a little, imbibed too much wine on occasion, and even come close to compromising a few young ladies. Then, his life had altered considerably after his parents' untimely death, and he was left alone. When he returned to an empty home aside from the servants, he realized it was time to assume the role and responsibility of a duke.

His business holdings had increased, securing his financial future for generations, save for that one tiny detail—the need for a wife by his thirtieth birthday. As the proposed wedding date drew nearer, would Willa become an eager companion to the arrangement, or should he cut his losses and search for a more *willing* replacement?

He stood, wiping his trousers with his palms. The decision was made. He would send for his lawyer that very day to amend the contract. In the meantime, he needed to discuss the changes with Middleton.

* * *

"This is a most unexpected announcement, Your Grace." Middleton wrung his hands before pouring himself a brandy. When he offered him a glass, James politely refused.

"I highly doubt the surprise. Your daughter has made it clear that marrying me is a repugnant notion and an unacceptable part of our financial agreement. I am making it easier for her to resume her position as mistress of Middleton Grange. As such, the household will remain unchanged and without further disruption. I only require a few more conditions." He approached the large desk and unfolded the paper with his demands. Middleton cleared his throat and further reviewed the contracts.

"N-no wedding? But, she would make a lovely duchess. I'm sure of that. She just needs time to warm to the idea."

"I do not believe that time would change her mind." Or her heart.

James withdrew to the window and stared out. Catching a glimpse of Willa wandering toward the garden, he lightly touched the breast pocket of his jacket. Her sketch crinkled under the fabric.

"I'll buy the farmland parcel. As you can see, it is a generous offer. That will allow you to pay D'Arby's debt yourself."

But I'd marry someone else...

"She'll come around. I know she will. Let's drink to that."

Middleton threw back the brandy in one long gulp, then swayed. "I think I'll have another."

James took the glass from Middleton's grasp. He shook his head to stop Willa's father from imbibing further. "I've considered it greatly. I cannot marry a woman so blatantly opposed to becoming the Duchess of Heighbury. But I will buy the outlying parcel of land which we agreed upon. You will save Middleton Grange and escape further harm from D'Arby."

James failed to mention that he had already sent the revised contract to his lawyer in London that afternoon. It gave him enough time to redraw the papers and return before the scheduled nuptials.

Middleton sank into a chair. "Should we ring for her then and deliver the news?"

James shook his head. "I'd much rather have the papers in hand so she can review them herself. That will give her the most peace and reassurance. As you stated, she requires calm and consistency. I wouldn't wish to distress her further."

"But the wedding preparations," Middleton began, rubbing his temples.

"Perhaps you can still hold a celebratory breakfast for the property sale." His eyes found Willa again as she strolled by a bed of tulips, running her hands over them. "And raise a toast to Willa's happiness, too," he murmured.

* * *

"I'M SO HAPPY," Willa exclaimed as she clapped her hands together. "Why didn't you tell me you were coming for a visit?"

"I wanted it to be a surprise," Cassandra answered, kissing her cousin's cheeks. It was highly irregular that her cousin should take so much time from her employers, but Lady Cronwell recently quit her London home to travel to Switzerland. Her husband, Lord Cronwell, remained in the city as Parliament remained in session.

"When she travels to Switzerland, Lady Cronwell prefers to employ a French-speaking companion to translate," she explained. "I am not fluent in foreign languages, you know." She spoke without a hint of jealousy or disappointment.

Willa pulled back from the embrace and squeezed her confidante's hands. "Then you have achieved your purpose. I'm positively thrilled to see you." Relief washed over her, knowing that she was no longer alone. She was hopeful that she could escape with Cassandra before her planned nuptials with James.

"I could scarcely believe the news when I received your letter. I had to come posthaste," Cassandra said, accepting a cup of tea. The women sat in the library, safely alone so they could converse in private.

Willa smoothed her skirt and sipped her drink. "Yes, I must apologize if I appeared too liberal in professing my feelings. As you can imagine, I was incensed by Papa's foolish business dealings. And his weakness for liquor." She frowned, now wishing she had not revealed so much. She loved her father dearly despite his shortcomings.

"You know, Cousin, you are much like him." She lowered her eyes from Willa's penetrating stare.

"Whatever do you mean?"

Cassandra set down her teacup and saucer.

"You are both hasty to act. His judgments concern business matters, colored with drink, while yours involve extreme reactions in uncontrollable situations. You both have a bit of temperament to manage." She reached for a teacake and popped it in her mouth.

Willa's lips parted in surprise at Cassandra's direct summation of her character, yet her words settled with a bit of sharp truth in them.

"You must know I am curious," her cousin continued after finishing the treat. "This man is a duke with money, and yet you do not wish to marry him?" She shook her head in confusion, her strawberry blonde curls bouncing.

"I am not interested in his station or what he is called." She flipped her wrist in a dismissive motion.

"Dearest Willa, we women do not have so many opportunities in life. As you know, I have fewer than you." She dipped her head, her signature move when she challenged Willa's views and feared a strong counter.

Willa pursed her lips. It was unfair yet true that her cousin would never rise above being a companion or vicar's wife if she continued down her life journey. With her current situation, it was far more reasonable to expect her to grow old working for another family unless she married a man likewise employed in service. For a man of prestige to rescue her from her station would be miraculous indeed. Cassandra would not hesitate to rejoice over her good fortune and embrace her rise in society.

"I am so at odds with myself, Cousin. Papa has incensed

me for his foolishness. But he is my only parent, and I love him dearly. I know he still suffers from the loss of Mama. Yet, he offers me like a gift to marry a duke so Middleton Grange can be saved."

She balled her fists. "The duke positively infuriates me with his cavalier conceit and shocking flirtations. To expect that I would be amenable to an arranged marriage with a complete stranger and forced out of my own home! I thought my family understood me." Relaxing her palms, she sighed. "However, sometimes I find myself drawn to him. He has a way of enticing my emotions until I simply do not know how to feel."

"How may I help you, dearest?"

She covered Cassandra's hand with her own. "Tell me I'm not foolish." The pleading in her voice softened Cassandra's expression.

"You want to marry for love, I presume."

Willa nodded. "If I cannot find employment in London and establish myself as independent, I should like to marry for more than just money." She wrinkled her nose.

Cassandra laughed. "Dearest Willa, I don't believe you understand what you would sacrifice to live as I do. And I don't believe you would pursue this dramatic scheme momentarily." She gestured to the elegant furnishings. "Independent I may seem, but one day Lady Cronwell won't be among the living, and then where shall I go? I must seek other employment. I have no idea if I will find another employer so generous." She shook her head.

Willa pursed her lips. Perhaps she hadn't thought of *that*.

"I believe you must consider your current option as the most sensible. Do you, *can you*, love this man?" Cassandra asked in a deliberate tone.

Before she could respond, a tremor overtook her hand,

and she pulled it away, tucking it under her skirt. Cassandra set her teacup down and leaned forward.

"Why are you trembling so, Cousin?"

Tears pricked Willa's eyes. She covered her face with a handkerchief and dabbed her eyelids.

"I don't know. It started some weeks ago. And I trip and fall over my feet. I think I'm just overwhelmed and need more rest."

Cassandra stood. "I'm calling for the doctor."

"No. Please wait. I do not wish to alarm Papa." She reached for Cassandra, but her cousin shrugged off her arm.

"This is not a negotiation, Willa. You must be examined immediately."

CHAPTER 7

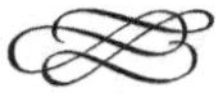

Sunlight streamed through the room, promising a day full of hopes and happiness. Willa stretched and yawned, feeling refreshed from the brandy the family physician, Doctor Martin, prescribed to induce a hardy sleep.

"Only drink this if you have exhausted every other method to gain sleep," he'd warned. Willa didn't need a reminder that her father indulged too much. She could understand after her fitful sleep why he preferred the drink, but she determined not to traverse down that road by repeating the ritual.

Willa blinked a few times before remembering his diagnosis. "You have *similar* symptoms of palsy," he had explained after examining her limbs and vitals. "But I highly doubt this is what's ailing you. You haven't experienced an incidence of stroke, and you're far too young. I recommend that you keep a diary to record the occurrences. It's more likely some deficiency of diet and a touch of anxiety over your upcoming nuptials.

"Nevertheless, let's keep an eye on it, shall we?" He

winked and promised to revisit after the proposed wedding. In the meantime, he further advised walks and exercise. "It is good for the body, soul, *and* spirit."

Eating healthy portions of mutton was also prescribed after she recounted the small amounts of food she had been ingesting lately. Her appetite had dwindled even more upon the dukes's arrival. Some of her gowns hung loosely on her usual Rubenesque frame, and Doctor Martin had tsked at her slender form.

At the mention of palsy, Aunt Rosamunde burst into tears, and her father disappeared, presumably to his study for a brandy. Cassandra remained at her bedside for the night. The duke, unaware of any disruptions in the household, rose early to the stables but returned too late to attend supper and meet Cassandra.

"Good morning, dear Cassandra. How did you sleep?" She stirred from the pastel damask settee situated close to the bed.

"I've slept better, but more importantly, how are you feeling?" She rested the back of her hand across Willa's forehead.

"I don't have a fever." She sat up in her large mahogany bed. "I feel perfectly rested."

Slipping out of bed, she pulled a robe about her shoulders and stretched her legs. Willa lowered herself at the dressing table, and her thoughts returned to the doctor's visit. Perhaps he held the key to her freedom. Would the duke enforce the contract or release them from their regrettable bind if she were truly ill with incurable and uncontrollable tremors?

"Should you be up and about just now?" Cassandra stood behind her and began brushing Willa's hair as she did when they were children.

Willa shook her head. "That is the first night in which I

have slept soundly. I do believe I'm eager to take on the day, whatever it may bring."

Her first thought upon hearing the presumptive diagnosis was that she was free. First, she was free from harboring the secret of her tremors and falls from her father and aunt. Second, His Grace couldn't possibly want to marry her now. He'd jump on his horse and gallop back to Heighbury Manor if even the tiniest hint of a disabling condition plagued her. The thought both satisfied and perturbed her.

Cassandra helped her dress, and then they headed down to breakfast. "When will I meet your bridegroom?" Cassandra asked as they linked arms and descended the stairs.

Willa cut a glance at her cousin. "He is not my bridegroom, and I cannot say when we'll make the introductions. I haven't caught a glimpse of him in days. He's hiding around here somewhere."

"Surely your father has not delivered the news of your health. I'm quite shocked he never appeared yesterday. Surely, he would show some concern." Cassandra glanced furtively around as if she expected the duke to jump out from behind the curtains.

"No, I'm sure he knows nothing of the matter." She patted her cousin's arm. "Please do not worry yourself. He is just a man." As she spoke, the words grew bitter on her tongue. He was not like any other man she had known. She missed his smile, teasing words, and how one lock of hair fell over his face when he spoke.

After a hearty breakfast, Cassandra begged for a stroll on the grounds.

"I'd be pleased to see your mother's rose garden again. And let's explore the hills as we did as children. Most days, my exercise entails climbing the dreadful stairs in the London townhouse." She linked arms with Willa, who hesitated. "Perhaps we'll catch a glimpse of your duke. Curiosity compels me."

Willa didn't want to be caught far from the house and take a tumble from shaking legs. She suggested they take a phaeton instead.

"I'll send for Charlie. He'll have us on our way quickly."

"No. That would ruin the experience. And the doctor said that exercise could be good for you." Cassandra secured her grip on Willa's arm and pulled her along.

"I believe the groom adores you still." Willa switched the subject to her cousin's childhood sweetheart.

Cassandra's pale complexion shifted to bright pink. "Don't be ridiculous. We were all great friends as children."

"Friends do not kiss." Willa wriggled her eyebrows up and down.

"It was on the cheek! And to stop me from crying over twisting my ankle."

Willa laughed freely at her cousin's embarrassment. She'd give anything for Cassandra to live full-time at the Grange. Middleton and the Buntlings had agreed to Cassandra's upbringing to include summers with Willa, learning the ways of polite society.

The close cousins walked for an hour, chatting and admiring the general splendor of nature until they reached the clearing at the edge of their estate. Willa gazed across the field and breathed deeply.

She tried to appear optimistic, but the remotest possibility that she had palsy threatened a downpour of depression.

I'll tell him tonight. James needs to know the whole truth so we can part ways amicably.

She explained to Cassandra that the stables would be included in the sale since they were rarely used. James had agreed to allow Middleton to keep his horses and carriage

there at no cost. It had been a sticking point once Willa found out.

As they headed to the house, the thunder of hoofbeats sounded in the distance. Willa spun around to see the duke galloping toward them.

James!

He pulled up close, tightening the reins as the horse neighed.

"Good morning, ladies." James tipped his hat but kept his eyes fixed on Willa.

Cassandra smiled widely and curtsied. She poked her cousin in the side with her finger.

"I haven't seen you of late. What have you been doing?" Willa's pulse quickened at the sight of him in his riding habit and great coat. It seemed an eternity since she'd seen him last. She had begun to wonder if she'd conjured up his existence. In their time apart, had he become even more handsome?

"Avoiding you, of course. Did you miss me?" She felt the heat on her face as his lips curved into a teasing smile. "I ride out every morning. It's a fetching piece of property." He hopped down from the horse, never taking his gaze from Willa's face. "It's beautiful, is it not?"

Property? Property! Surely, he doesn't mean me. Emotions waged war within her as Cassandra linked their arms.

"Aren't you going to introduce us?" He tipped his head in Cassandra's direction.

"Of course," and Willa quickly made proper introductions.

Cassandra asked, "Will you join us for tea this afternoon, Your Grace?"

"I'd be delighted. But only if Willa permits me," he offered with little humor.

Willa wanted to reach out and smooth a wave of hair

peeking from the brim of his beaver hat, then recalled propriety. Instead, she fiddled with the ribbons of her bonnet.

"Yes, please join us," she said, offering a curtsy.

"Wonderful." He tugged the brim of his hat and remounted his horse.

Wonderful, indeed. Observing James atop the horse, exuding all sorts of masculinity, only muddled her thoughts further.

CHAPTER 8

"Wilhemina, if you don't marry that man, I will throw my bonnet his way," Cassandra threatened good-naturedly. "He's a nonpareil and clearly wild with love for you."

Willa scoffed, pinching Cassandra in the arm for her lack of modest summation. "He is not. I'm a business transaction to him. But I'm going to break it."

"Why? *When?*"

"After tea. I will tell him about my tremors and release him from his promise. He won't want to marry me after I confess my illness. But I will urge Papa to sell him the parcel. I am the only part of the contract that would nullify the situation."

"But you mustn't, Willa. It would mislead him to a false conclusion. Remember, the doctor warned you not to be too hasty in your assumptions. He only said it mimicked palsy, but not definitely. I feel certain that he is correct." She nodded in assurance.

"And if it is something dire? What can I offer a man of wealth and title? I'm sure I could not, nay, should not bear children. But if I did, would I leave them just as Mama left me?"

"Your mama did not die of palsy but from a tragic fall from a horse."

Willa remembered bitterly her mama's slow, agonizing death as she slipped away into unconsciousness, eventually succumbing to a head injury. Her father prohibited her from riding horses after her mother's death, but such an order never stopped Willa from visiting the stables.

The clop-clop of horse hooves neared them. Willa knew it was James returning; the thought made her smile.

"I thought you ladies might enjoy an escort back to the house," he offered, pulling up alongside them.

"Your Grace, what a surprise. Ten minutes have not passed since we last met. Are we in a race? If we are, you have the upper hand. I am sure we could not outrun your stallion."

Cassandra's light-hearted banter stirred feelings of jealousy in Willa. She frowned. Why couldn't she be so light and carefree, especially with gentlemen? Her discourse with the opposite sex had always been considered dispassionate. She'd been unable to do anything but wait like a footman for something romantic or exciting to happen, which it never did.

None of the gentlemen, including James, asked her to dance at the few balls she'd attended. She usually found herself stuck in conversation with an old married man sporting a portly middle, indulging in too much drink. After two Seasons of enduring such rejection, she'd begged her father not to take her.

James laughed at Cassandra's question. "I am in a race against the calendar, for in just eight days, I must convince Miss Middleton to be my wife."

Cassandra chortled. "Then you will have to speed your

plans. I have heard on good authority from the book of Ephesians that the days are evil."

James leaned over the horse and offered his hand to Willa. "Then we must not postpone a moment longer. Join me for a ride, Willa."

Willa's head snapped up quickly. "You can't mean for me to come up with you." Her eyes widened in fear. Her pulse quickened, and her lips tingled at the thought of such close contact with him.

"I do, indeed. Plenty of room in the saddle with me." James winked. "Lightning here is quite gentle and loves the ladies. We'll ride to that tree in the distance at an easy canter." He pointed to an old oak situated five hundred yards away.

Willa paused and followed his gaze to the tree. She hadn't been on a horse in ages and, as an unmarried woman, was bound to her Papa's rules.

She shook her head and stepped back. "I couldn't possibly. My father doesn't allow me to ride. Not to mention that it would be entirely too improper."

"I'll go if you won't," Cassandra murmured. Willa knew her cousin was teasing, but it riled her the same.

"Then help me." Shaking off the fear of riding, she extended her hand as James freed his foot from the stirrup so hers could slip inside the loop.

After a few tries with Cassandra pushing her up, she succeeded as James assisted her in settling in front of his saddle on the withers. She swore her cousin to secrecy. Not only were they breaking the rules of propriety but also her father's command.

"Now, just lean against me," he whispered, sending her heart racing as he clasped his arm firmly about her waist. Willa had never been so intimately close to a man before.

Opening her mouth to protest, she clamped it shut as the horse jolted forward into a trot.

She squealed at the unexpected movement. James squeezed her midsection tightly with one arm as he held the reigns with his other hand.

"I won't let you fall. I promise," James whispered, his breath tickling her cheek.

But his words came too late. She was already falling for the duke.

CHAPTER 9

When they returned to the house, James excused himself to inquire about the post. Finding no deliveries addressed to him, he paced the hall. The papers from his lawyer in London should have already arrived by express.

"Won't you join us for tea?" Mrs. Livingston appeared with a thin smile.

His eyes drank in Willa's form as they neared the drawing room. Her cheeks still flushed from exercise, Willa had coiled her hair into a neat knot at her nape. She'd exchanged her sea-foam green colored cotton gown with a white muslin and lace that bordered her throat. She greeted him, her color still high.

If she was attempting to dissuade him from thoughts of marriage, Willa was failing miserably.

Earlier, she'd confessed she hadn't ridden in years. It astonished and pleased him that she'd confronted her fear in such a decisive manner. Feeling her form press against him, the instinct to protect Willa surged through his being.

How strange that she hadn't been on a horse for a long

time with the fully stocked stable on the grounds. She'd picked up riding sidesaddle quite well, and James was anxious to take her out again on her own horse. Once he released her, she could ride as freely as she pleased on the grounds, including the parcel he would own. Protectiveness swelled within his chest.

Once they'd finished their tea, Willa approached him and suggested they walk in the garden. Cassandra followed, leaving a respectful distance.

"I hope I'm not being too forward, but it is imperative that I speak with you, Your Grace."

As she addressed him formally once again, he set his jaw. After their enjoyment that afternoon, he had hoped she would put away all formalities.

Arm in arm, he guided her to a bench where they had spoken that first day. Now, James was afraid to hope that her heart might be opening for him to fill with his love.

Love. He shook his head in annoyance. He hadn't set out to love her, only marry her as part of the arrangement with Middleton. His lips thinned in irritation.

Blasted D'Arby. Once the entire matter was settled, he'd never receive that scamp in his home—or his life—again. Fully realizing this was his motive for releasing her from their bargain, his heart beat with regret over how meeting Willa had come about. Thank heavens she wasn't privy to all the details of that fateful night when her future and home had been gambled away. The thought of entering another gentlemen's club for the foolish purpose of squandering what the Lord had blessed him with churned his stomach.

"I have something to confess, Your Grace."

"Please, call me James. We are alone now."

"James." Her face softened. "I must confess something difficult. An unexpected discovery has plagued me this day. I cannot delay a moment longer to deliver the news."

He took her hands. Perhaps he was mistaken. Were her feelings changed, and was she more affectionate toward him?

"You can tell me anything, Willa." Now that they were on the edge of mutual affirmation, he took the liberty of brushing her fingers across his lips.

James cursed himself for revising the contract. It would make no difference. They would marry, Willa would be secure in her future, and there would be love for a lifetime. He wanted their children to have her eyes. And his hair. Oh, who cared? They would be a beautiful reflection of them both.

Willa gently pulled her hands from his. The same hand began trembling as it had done before. She stared down at them as he waited for an explanation.

"What is the matter, my darling?" He tipped her chin up.

Her lips trembled. *"This* is the matter." She held the affected hand to him. "While you were away yesterday, the doctor examined me."

As the words tumbled out, she covered her face with her hands.

Fear gripped his heart. So, this is what she needed to tell him. He braced himself for whatever news may come next.

"He says I *may* have palsy." At her confession, she covered her face with a handkerchief.

"May have? He isn't certain?" Palsy had taken the life of an older uncle. She was too young for this diagnosis. And her tremors had not raised a suspicion of the same disease in him.

After she had quietened, she explained the doctor was unsure but would be visiting again in a week to do more tests. *Well, that is good news.* His uncle had been diagnosed immediately and succumbed to a severe fall shortly after.

"Nothing is certain, but no one knows how severe my condition may be or become. As you can see, I cannot marry you. But please honor the sale to Papa. He will need some sort of trust for my aunt. You would do me that kindness, wouldn't you?" Her hazel eyes implored him for sympathy.

James stiffened as though she had struck him. Why had Willa encouraged his affections moments before, if only to discard him?

Just like Genevieve. The betrayal between his former betrothed and D'Arby continued to sting despite the time that had passed. At first, he'd believed Willa to be honest, even if it meant she sometimes behaved without emotional restraint. How could he have been so foolish?

He rose to his feet and stared into the fish pond. "No, I will not." His eyes followed the fish as they made graceful laps about their sanctuary. Wheeling around to face her, he demanded to speak to the doctor. "When I hear from him that you are certain to be dying, I will consider your counter-proposal. Until then, we will be married one week from tomorrow, or your father will lose everything."

"Leave me then. I shall have no peace until you release my family from this hopeless entanglement." Her voice broke, and she collapsed against the bench.

He regarded her for a moment. Willing her to look at him, she lifted her head.

"Please," she whispered. Her demeanor shifted again as she extended a gloved hand.

"Miss Middleton, I am genuinely sorry for your worry. Please understand I haven't the appetite to dine here tonight." He bowed slightly to Miss Lawton, then left Willa again.

* * *

James gripped the banister, his heart and legs heavy from Willa's crushing blow. She had misled him with her emotional pendulum. Why couldn't she trust him? Hadn't he proven himself sincere enough? How could he have such raw luck with women?

"Your Grace, excuse me, but this letter came for you by express not half an hour ago." James looked up to see his valet, Barnaby, holding a letter.

He grabbed the edge as if it might burn him and fled to his room. Breaking the seal, he quickly scanned the contents.

Very well. Willa would have her freedom and be released from an unwanted marriage after all.

CHAPTER 10

The girls locked arms and walked to town. Willa needed a new bonnet, according to Cassandra.

"For your trousseau," she explained with a wink.

"There will not be a honeymoon if I can help it." She sighed, admiring the many bolts of fabric and bonnet designs.

"Then I need new ribbons for my bonnet with all the suitors lining up outside my door." Cassandra pursed her lips.

"What about Charlie?" Willa smirked, happy to turn the attention away from her ordeal with James.

Cassandra's ivory complexion paled further. "Please stop your teasing, Cousin. He's a nice boy, but he's only a groom."

Willa tsked. "He is a hard worker, loyal to a fault, and quite handsome. I've seen how he steals glances at you when you're not looking. I think he's a fine catch for—"

"For someone like me?" Cassandra finished her sentence.

"I didn't mean—" She bit her lip.

"You'd be right. Our stations are hardly to be strived for, but there's someone for everyone."

"Not everyone." Willa sighed as she twirled ribbons between her fingers. "I informed *him* about palsy last night, and he refused to allow me out of the contract like a true gentleman would." She bit the inside of her cheek, a childhood habit that Aunt Rosamunde had tried without success to break.

"Willa, that is deceitful even for you. You know the doctor believes it to be something mild with your diet. You should have been forthright with him, no matter your personal feelings. Why would you agree to come to the milliners if you thought yourself truly ill?"

"I needed out of the house."

Cassandra pulled her into a corner of the shop. After a quick greeting to the milliner, her cousin chastised her. "The physician said he does not think you have palsy, Wilhemina. If I were supposed to marry the duke, I would likely tremble from happiness. And what was that whole bit riding with him on the horse?"

"But if it's even a possibility, he should know. Wouldn't you want to know if you had a wife who might be ill? Besides, I haven't consented to the marriage." She examined a bonnet on display when a few prying eyes of other customers followed their direction.

"I like this one," Cassandra announced to feed the gossips. "It's a lovely white and will go well with your trousseau. The duke will approve."

Gasps and whispers echoed across the shop. A tall, striking woman with blonde curls under a leghorn hat adorned with peacock feathers approached Willa and her cousin.

"Pardon me for interrupting, but did you mention a *duke*?" Her melodious voice sang like a bird, but her glinting eyes hinted at another tune.

"Why, yes. My cousin is marrying the Duke of Heighbury." Cassandra lifted her chin a tad higher than usual. Willa nudged her. Her cousin never behaved so petty and proud.

"My, my. It seems I've found the woman who stole my James's heart." Her sapphire eyes darkened to cobalt in an instant.

Cassandra made the introductions while Willa grasped the woman's words. She introduced herself as Lady Genevieve Waterford of Brighton.

"You say you know the duke?"

"Indeed, I do. There was a time when I fancied I would be the next Duchess of Heighbury." She flicked her eyes over Willa's plain pink muslin dress, modestly buttoned to her neck.

Lady Genevieve dressed to be noticed, but Willa rarely paid attention to fashion, until now. As she surveyed the woman's appearance, Lady Genevieve seemed ready for any occasion in a lavender spencer jacket with black velvet brocade. As a man and a duke, James would find the woman's appearance arresting. Willa felt herself lacking next to this poised and comely creature.

"How exactly did you come to be acquainted with the duke?" Lady Genevieve's eyes narrowed.

"I, well…" Willa debated how to answer.

Lady Genevieve stepped closer, towering over Willa's slight frame.

The words that formed in her mind would not make their way out of her mouth.

"They were matched by her father, Sir Edgar Middleton," Cassandra offered.

"Indeed. That explains *so* much." Lady Genevieve eyed Willa.

Without a word, Willa gathered her skirts, curtsied, and hurried out the door. When she'd reached the end of the line of shops, Cassandra caught up to her, begging her to stop. "What are you doing, Cousin?" she asked, out of breath.

"Don't you see? That was the woman James—the duke—should have married. I cannot compete with a lady of her caliber." Willa's eyes pricked with tears. She pulled a handkerchief from her reticule and dabbed at them.

Cassandra put an arm around her shoulders. "Why would another lady's former claims disturb you so much if you weren't inclined to marry him then, dearest?"

Cassandra's question stopped her in her tracks.

"You don't understand. It isn't just her. It's her sort. She is an absolute sculpture, so tall and majestic. Here I am, absolutely ordinary, with short legs and clumsy feet. Not one gentleman has ever looked my way twice."

"Except for the handsome Duke of Heighbury, you mean. His eyes shine when he looks your way. And mind you not to be so proud and conceited, Cousin. *'A woman of noble character is worth more than many rubies.'*"

"Please don't lecture me on inner beauty from the Proverbs, Cassandra. I would highly prefer being beautiful than ordinary."

"Perhaps it would do you some good to speak with the vicar. He could provide you with the guidance you need." She nudged Willa as they approached the church.

Pangs of guilt constricted her throat. This whole affair was a disaster. If she agreed to marry James, Middleton Grange would be saved, and her father and aunt would continue their lives without disruption. She would be uprooted from a predictable life caring for her father to answering to a man who may break her heart. Yet, she would be well taken care of.

Should she break her part of the agreement, the world she knew would fall apart in a different manner. They would have no home, plunge in rank, and only Providence knew what may befall them. She may as well join Cassandra in service.

And James should no doubt marry the beautiful and elegant Lady Genevieve.

Perhaps Cassandra was correct in her ideas. She should speak with their vicar, Mr. Brown, soon. His sermons always offered a balm to her spirit.

CHAPTER 11

"You have a visitor, miss."

Willa and Cassandra looked up from their needlework in unison. They passed the day in the sitting room as a thunderstorm had ruined any plans out of doors. Willa's eyebrows shot up as she took the calling card from the footman. She frowned.

"Who is it, Cousin?"

"Lady Genevieve," Willa grumbled.

"How very strange to be calling in this weather," Cassandra commented as she focused on her needlework. "And so soon after meeting her yesterday."

Taking deep breaths, Willa addressed the footman. "Show her to the drawing room, please. And tell the kitchen we have a guest and shall need more tea."

"It could be the perfect opportunity to clarify her relationship with James," Cassandra suggested.

"He's out riding again," Willa said, her voice hollow of enthusiasm.

"In this weather? Goodness, I hope not. He'll catch his death out there."

Willa gripped her stitching. She hadn't thought of that. Since arriving at Middleton Grange, he rode the property nearly daily. It had become a ritual, leaving Willa to her blessed solitude. She'd been so absorbed in her own troubles that she hadn't considered the possibility that he might be in danger.

"Come now, dearest. We must receive your visitor as propriety dictates. I'm sure the duke is safe wherever he might be." She rolled her eyes.

Willa followed her cousin to the drawing room. Upon entering, they caught Lady Genevieve running a gloved fingertip along the fireplace.

After a quick curtsy between the women, the sparring began.

"Good afternoon, Miss Middleton. I'm sure you are curious as to my unexpected visit. I'm visiting relations in Guildford. How fortuitous that I should be so close to your home." Lady Genevieve sat on the divan and spread her skirts over the cushions.

"The weather is quite formidable today, keeping most callers at home." Her gaze traveled to the window where black skies loomed. The rain had stopped, but the foreboding clouds promised an encore.

It's as dark and gloomy outside as inside my heart.

She studied Lady Genevieve. Of course, even in the darkest storms, she would shine bright as the sun, dressed in a canary yellow pelisse and matching bonnet. Lady Genevieve removed her gloves carefully and set them in her lap. "I hope you forgive my frankness, but I needed to see this arrangement—I mean, James—for myself. You see, it's quite unconscionable that he is betrothed so quickly after our understanding." She cast a knowing look at Willa, who raised an eyebrow at the woman's brash statement.

"What understanding might that be?" Cassandra asked

tartly. Willa smiled with gratitude for her cousin's sudden bravado as her mind fumbled with what to say next. As she studied their guest, a rush of protectiveness washed over her. If this woman came to claim her James, she would have to do better than evade the issue.

"Cousin, would you mind fetching my shawl? I feel a slight draft." She shivered as if to accentuate the chill.

Cassandra's eyes widened at Willa. Offering a brief curtsy to Lady Genevieve, she left the room, firmly shutting the door behind her.

"Now that we're alone, what do you wish to tell me, Lady Genevieve? I find directness a desirable character trait." Stupid, she was not. Despite her lack of regular social interaction beyond the Grange, Willa understood perfectly when a woman had something to say.

Lady Genevieve smiled, her eyes darkening.

"Since you've asked kindly, I have some information I believe you'll find quite useful." Her bow-shaped lips twisted into a sneer.

Willa clasped her hands together in her lap, waiting for the ominous disclosure.

"Are you acquainted with Sir Lawrence D'Arby of London?"

"I am not."

Lady Genevieve cocked her head to one side. "I suppose a woman of your standing would not be familiar with a man of his reputation."

"What of this man? Should I know him?"

"That depends entirely on if you wish to know of his *acquaintance* with the duke."

Willa's head snapped up at the reference to James. "Please, enlighten me."

"If you are certain—"

"I haven't all afternoon to wait for your disclosure. Who knows who else might visit on a stormy day such as this?"

Ignoring Willa's impatience, Lady Genevieve launched a detailed account of James and Sir Lawrence's boyhood escapades at Eton, leading to their adult gambling.

"I fail to see the significance of this information. Many men attend the gaming tables. My father included." Willa's patience thinned. She stood, praying Lady Genevieve would understand the movement as an invitation to leave.

"I'm not quite finished, Miss Middleton. Pray, sit down."

As Lady Genevieve continued her monologue, she disclosed the next layer of news.

"What do you mean my father owes Sir Lawrence money?"

A commotion in the hall drew their attention toward the door. Willa and Lady Genevieve exchanged glances when they recognized James's voice.

Lady Genevieve stood, her gloves slipping to the floor. A footman entered and summoned Willa.

"Excuse me, miss. The duke desires a word."

Willa followed, not feeling her legs as she exited. When she appeared in the hall, James took her by the arm.

"Shall we move to the library?" the duke suggested but had already half-dragged her to the room.

"You're dripping wet, Your Grace," Willa said, her words above a whisper. He had forgotten to remove his hat and cloak.

"I am quite in the middle of a morning call—Lady Genevieve Waterford of Brighton. I do believe you have the honor of having made her acquaintance. Now, is there an emergency that you wish to pull me away from my guest?" she asked, not daring to meet his eyes.

James paced the room. "I know she's here. I saw her carriage. What the deuce is going on?"

"I'm not sure what you mean."

"I'm quite certain that you do. Now, tell me. What has she told you?" He approached her carefully, taking her hands in his.

Willa only shook her head, willing away the tears that stung her eyes.

"Willa, please. I implore you. What has she said to you?"

Slowly, she met his eyes. "Nothing of importance. An exchange in greeting. She only arrived five minutes ago."

"I can see something has shaken you."

Willa pursed her lips together. She couldn't bear to repeat Lady Genevieve's cautioning words, fearing they would come true.

"I know nothing." She wriggled her arms to break his grasp, but his grip tightened.

"Then why is there torment behind your eyes?" he asked tenderly.

At that moment, she fought the urge to crumble under him. How could a man with enough strength to crush her with his hands be so gentle with the same touch?

* * *

James pulled her face close, forcing her to look at him. "Willa, please."

Her breath tickled his chin as she allowed him to pull her closer until their lips almost touched. An inch closer, and he would ravage her with kisses. It was inevitable. They had danced around the attraction for too long.

Willa looked away, her lower lip quivering.

"Am I so disgusting to you?" he whispered. If Willa sincerely disliked him, he would leave the estate immediately. He could not bear it if she held no warm feelings toward him, contract or not.

James felt her shiver under his touch. Her eyes half-closed in surrender, and she shook her head.

Her lips parted slightly as an invitation to come closer when a firm knock at the door startled them both.

"Perfect timing," James muttered as he stepped aside.

"James! What a surprise," Lady Genevieve purred. She slinked over to him and offered her hand.

He responded with a quick bow, then stepped back.

"Always the gentleman," Lady Genevieve answered, her gaze moving over Willa. "You should join us for tea. Miss Middleton, I believe they have replenished your tea tray." She looped an arm through his and steered him away from Willa. James stopped shy of the door.

"Willa?" His mouth still burned from the near touch of hers.

Willa smoothed her chemisette and patted her hair. James caught the motion of her trembling fingers. He cocked his head to the side, unsure whether the movement stemmed from her mysterious ailment or emotions. In response, her cheek color deepened several pink shades.

Perhaps all is not lost.

Cassandra burst through the door with Willa's shawl in hand. "Oh! Here you all are." She gave James a quick curtsy. "When Lady Genevieve quit the room to take some air, I didn't realize she was going to explore *all* the rooms." She raised an eyebrow.

"Nonsense. If I had known the duke would be joining us for tea, I would have dressed for the occasion." She twirled slightly, showing off her expensive garment.

They withdrew toward the drawing room to resume tea. James stopped in the hall and pulled Willa aside.

"Whatever information she has disclosed to you, I

promise to explain later." He pressed his fingers into her arm. As she removed his hand, hers began to tremble. This time, there was no mistaking the tremor.

"Willa," he began, eyeing her hand. She nodded once and followed Cassandra.

Resigning himself to being outnumbered, James joined the ladies for an afternoon of interrogation.

CHAPTER 12

Willa tapped her foot while Edith fastened her pelisse in place. She hadn't visited London since her last Season, but the errand for which she readied herself was paramount to the future of Middleton Grange.

"My dear, where are you off to in such finery at this hour?" Aunt Rosamunde entered, still in her dressing gown. "Shouldn't you be asleep?"

Willa pulled her gloves on. She must present herself as elegantly as possible if she were to be taken seriously. "I am for London. On an errand."

"What sort of errand? This is highly irregular. Is Cassandra returning now? Before your wedding?"

Willa had considered asking her cousin along but decided the less anyone knew of her plans, the better. "She is not. I-I have an obligation I must tend to." Edith helped her with her bonnet, but Aunt Rosamunde stopped Willa as she approached the door.

"Pray, what sort of obligation? Is it to do with the wedding?"

Willa pursed her lips. Her aunt was nothing if not

shrewd. She could outrun her aunt to the carriage, which would not be difficult. Or she could confide in Aunt Rosamunde and trust she would act as a cover.

She had just selected the first choice when her aunt drew so near she could feel her breath on her forehead.

Very well.

She would reveal her mission to London, releasing them all from the contract, and pray that Aunt Rosamunde would be a willing co-conspirator. "In a sense, it has everything to do with the wedding." She dismissed Edith. "I have discovered the identity of the person responsible for the situation that has placed our home in its current turmoil." She stepped back from her aunt and waited for the argument to begin.

"But the duke is here, my love."

Willa shook her head. "You misunderstand me. Another person holds the key to my freedom from this farce. And he is the one to free us from losing Middleton Grange."

"How do you mean?" Aunt Rosamunde lowered herself on Willa's bed.

"I have it on good authority that the person to whom Papa owes money is not the duke but another man. I intend to speak with him and undo the damage. I've been assured he's quite reasonable."

The plan seemed like a good idea when Willa had thought it up. As she spoke, her words revealed a desperate female recklessly determined on a desperate mission to confront Sir Lawrence alone. Of course, she would not put herself into such a questionable situation without full contemplation. She hoped her aunt would see that as well.

"Listen to me, young lady." Her aunt wagged a finger in her face. "You will not under any circumstances pursue this matter. It stops right here. We will rouse your father and the duke and end this ridiculous charade immediately."

"I must go, Aunt! I have not a moment to lose. I cannot

allow this man to hold our family hostage." She cut her eyes at Aunt Rosamunde and stood her ground. If her aunt wouldn't fight for the family, the responsibility fell on Willa's shoulders.

To her surprise, her aunt relented.

"I assume you plan for the duke to accompany you."

Willa lifted her chin, determined to follow through with the journey without his knowledge.

"Charlie and Edith will attend me. Papa is to know nothing of this." She summoned Edith and asked her to send for the undergroom.

"Foolish girl." Aunt Rosamunde cast Willa a long, hard look. "You realize with your actions that you will ruin your reputation and the reputation of this family."

"Oh, Aunt Rosamunde. My heart is already ruined."

* * *

Willa set her shoulders. Indeed, the man would be reasonable. She would explain that her father hadn't been prudent with business matters for quite some time. If necessary, she would further clarify that he had made a misstep after her mother's death, and grief was the primary cause. Yes, that would do.

"Shouldn't I come in with you, miss?" Edith glanced furtively around, unfamiliar with London. The address had led them to an office building in a suspicious part of London.

"Please remain here with Charlie. I am confident that my meeting will go according to plan. He's a businessman. Therefore, I believe him to be a sensible person. Wait here, please. I shan't be long." Her gaze wandered up the building. If the man worked the Exchange as Lady Genevieve had promised, it stood to reason that they would arrive home unscathed.

On second thought, perhaps having her maid near in case she needed assistance would be wise. She asked Edith to accompany her.

Within, they ascended the four flights of stairs to an open area. A single set of doors to the left greeted them. She approached and knocked softly at first.

"Please wait here, Edith. If I'm not back in five minutes, summon help."

Hearing a man and woman's laughter on the other side, Willa stood back to confirm the number a second time. Yes, she was in the right place.

She knocked louder, and the laughter stopped, followed by excited whispers. Waiting a few moments longer, she nearly decided defeat when the door swung open. A dark-haired woman dressed in a long hooded cape exited, closing the door behind her.

"Excuse me, is this the office of Sir Lawrence D'Arby?"

The woman scowled. "Aye. Ye better be quick about it. I 'ad meself an appointment that ye interrupted."

Willa started from the woman's demeanor. The woman leaned toward her and hissed. "Make sure 'e pays ye for yer trouble." With that, her cloaked figure swished down the stairs, grumbling at each step.

After the door below clicked behind the woman, Willa knocked a third time.

Heavy footsteps approached and swung the door open wide. "I told you, Miss Little, I'll pay when you finish—" Realizing that Willa was not Miss Little, the man straightened his jacket. "Well. And who might you be?" His gaze moved over Willa's form. Ignoring his leer, Willa curtsied.

"Good afternoon, sir. I'm here to see Sir Lawrence D'Arby."

He peered at her intently. "Who may I say is calling?"

"I am Miss Wilhemina Middleton, sir. Of Middleton Grange."

Rather than bow, the man let out a sharp hoot. "Come in, Miss Middleton." She took a few steps inside the office and then lost her courage. Perhaps this wasn't a good idea. As she made her way to leave, he blocked her with his towering form and closed the door. Leaning against it, he crossed his arms.

"I am the man you seek. Please, have a seat." He gestured to a chair inside. "Care for a drink?"

Panic filled Willa's senses. She should have listened to Aunt Rosamunde and stayed home.

"No, thank you. Forgive me, sir. I have made a grave mistake. Good day." She waited for him to step away from the door. Instead, he moved toward her. Willa froze.

He dropped his smile and then strode to the large oak desk that occupied most of the room. Papers lay strewn across the top. The faint scent of Miss Little's perfume lingered in the air.

"You may sit." He folded his hands and waited, his eyes penetrating her own.

She hesitated briefly before lowering herself on the chair. Perching on the edge, she readied herself to spring up at a moment's notice.

Silence passed between them for several seconds. He leaned back, waiting for her to initiate the reason for her visit. She had come this far. She may as well have her say and then depart posthaste.

"You see, sir, I received your name and address from a Lady Genevieve—"

"Ha! Indeed. And how is Lady Genevieve these days? It has been some time since I've had the *pleasure* of her company."

Willa's skin prickled at his words. She prayed that Edith was on her way to fetch Charlie to escort her back home. She would be out of here shortly if all went as she'd rehearsed.

"She is well and sends her regards." Willa swallowed, but the lump in her throat grew by the moment. "As I was saying, I have come to relay some information that you may find useful about the business agreement between you and my father, Sir Edgar Middleton."

The words tumbled out. Willa had promised herself she would not become emotional. She would not cry. If he were a reasonable man, as Lady Genevieve reassured, she could bargain with him.

"Ah, yes. And how is your papa?" He drummed his fingertips together.

"He is very well, thank you."

"And your betrothed?" Sir Lawrence smirked.

Willa hesitated. If she admitted they were engaged, her visit would be in vain. The point was to extricate herself and her family from the situation. But at least the man would know she was protected, and he would not make any unwanted advances for risk of retaliation. That much she knew of James. He would never allow her to be hurt, whether they married or not.

At that moment, she wished he were by her side more than anything. From the moment she'd discovered Sir Lawrence's involvement, she'd tried to understand how James had become involved in this debacle. More importantly, why had she been warned that she must marry him to secure the family home? Whatever the reason, intimacy and understanding had planted in her heart for James despite her unwillingness to be snatched from the comfort and safety of the home that bore memories of her beloved mama.

Weighing her options, she decided honesty was best

when dealing with a man of business. "If you refer to the duke, I'm afraid we are not engaged, sir."

Sir Lawrence tsked. "I'm surprised to hear it. I had heard rumors otherwise." His lips contorted into a wicked smile.

"You see, he came to us with a proposal of which I know you are aware, but it did not meet the standards or expectations of the intended arrangement."

Sir Lawrence rose and moved around the desk. He leaned against it, his thigh touching Willa's arm. "You speak in riddles. What sort of standards meet your approval, Miss Middleton?"

Willa scooted back into the chair, away from his touch. "I mean to say that this situation is absurd."

"Why is that?" Sir Lawrence leaned over and placed his hands on both arms of the chair, attempting to block Willa from standing.

"You cannot force my father to enter an agreement so ridiculous. He is a grieving widower who mistakenly entered into this business contract."

Sir Lawrence leaned back and folded his hands. "Your father knowingly put up his entire estate for financial risk. If he lost, perhaps he should be kept at home, away from the temptation of gambling with his property and with your future. Not to mention from the brandy he's so terribly fond of."

Willa stood. "How dare you, sir! He has not been in his right mind since my mother died. You can hardly hold him accountable for one foolish occasion of imbibing too much in public and making ridiculous agreements. Release him at once."

Sir Lawrence's mouth contorted with cold fury. "Miss Middleton, you realize that your duke is the man who saved your father from his agreement with *me*. Well, once your end of the bargain has been fulfilled. The duke needs a wife. Have you asked him about that part of the agreement?"

Willa's hand fluttered to her heart. "W-what are you saying? Lady Genevieve said—"

He held a hand up. "Sir Edgar and I had the original agreement. That is true. But the duke was present and offered to pay *me* to satisfy the debt on your father's behalf so long as your beloved papa agreed to allow him to buy the parcel. Your father pays Heighbury. He pays me. All is well and satisfied. And the duke keeps his estate so long as he is married by his next birthday, which happens to be, oh, next week."

The complete revelation of James's motives for marrying her splintered her heart. So, that was the truth behind his insistence upon them marrying. He needed her to hold onto his family fortune.

Every flirtatious remark James had ever spoken cycled through her thoughts. Each appreciative look and his light, teasing touch stripped her mind bare of hope that he loved her. Understanding his motives completed the picture that had been unfinished.

"I know that look, Miss Middleton. Allow me to reassure you that you were not completely used ill. I do believe the duke has developed a *tendre* for you. In fact, he nearly threatened to plant a facer on me because of you."

Willa searched his face for a hint of deception but found none.

"Who knows? Perhaps he's fooled us both." The tiny sliver of hope he offered disappeared in a sneer. "If I know the duke, he thrives on winning whatever is at stake, especially with his estate at risk." He trailed a finger along her arm. "Your papa threw you in for good measure. Too bad His Grace couldn't win you over. Perhaps I should have made that part of the arrangement with your father instead."

Willa froze under his dark expression. She had to escape now or risk further unsavory advances.

He must have read her thoughts. As she moved to sprint to the exit, his arm caught her. He yanked her against his chest. "What about it, Miss Middleton? If a duke isn't good enough for you, perhaps I am."

His hands ran roughly over the front of her pelisse, and he yanked it open. He pushed her to the floor and forced his mouth on her neck. She swiveled her head away from the stench of tobacco and liquor on his breath. Willa tried to scream, but fear clogged her throat, eliciting only a gurgle.

Sir Lawrence clamped a hand on her mouth and warned her not to scream. Tears flowed freely down Willa's cheeks. She would rather perish in the street like a dog than come home a ruined woman. James's face flashed before her, and she squeezed her eyelids together, regretting every ill-tempered word she'd used with him. She'd do anything to escape this terror.

As his hands made contact with her petticoat, she felt his weight lift off her in a swift motion. Instinctively, she tugged the hem of her garments to cover herself and rolled over. Someone else was in the room. A man grunted in conjunction with thudding sounds.

Strong arms pulled her from the floor. "Get out of here now!" the voice demanded.

Willa wiped the back of her mouth with her sleeve, focusing on the door. Just a few steps to freedom, she turned to see James holding Sir Lawrence against the wall by his collar.

CHAPTER 13

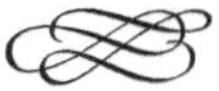

Willa perched in the window seat of her bedchamber as she waited for James. It had been hours since Charlie and Edith escorted her home from the coaching inn between Surrey and London—hours since she'd left him as he knelt over Sir Lawrence D'Arby with a raised fist. The man had behaved criminally and nearly ruined her when James burst through the door, saving her from what atrocity she shivered to imagine.

Had he hurt him? Killed him? Her mind sought answers should the authorities come calling. James had saved her life and her virtue. Now, she had the opportunity to save him.

Lost in thought, she nearly missed the sound of approaching hooves. Wrapping her dressing gown tightly about her, she hurried out into the courtyard to find James handing over his horse to Charlie.

"Willa," he said, throwing down his hat and taking her in his arms. "Are you alright?" His breath was warm against her face. Her heart raced.

With a growing knot in her throat, she nodded. "Now that you're here, how can I not be?"

He stroked her hair from her face, and she sank further into his embrace.

"You are never to go to London without a proper chaperone or near that libertine again. D'Arby is the worst kind of reprobate. If he'd hurt you, if I hadn't come in when I did . . ." His voice broke as his words trailed. "He's lucky I didn't kill him."

Willa clung to him, relieved he hadn't killed the rogue. She tilted her head back and placed her palm against his cheek.

"Did you hurt him?" she asked, swallowing the shame in her throat.

"He has a few bruises to explain, but I wouldn't risk being parted from you by inflicting further harm."

"How did you know where I'd gone?" In the end, it didn't matter. Still, she was grateful he'd appeared when she needed him.

"Your aunt. She may have promised not to tell your father, but she didn't make the same promise to me. Whatever could you have been thinking to involve yourself with such treachery?"

"When Lady Genevieve visited, she revealed that Sir Lawrence held the means to release us all from the arrangement. She *promised* he was a man of honor. Despite your previous engagement, she swore she was trying to help—"

"Herself. The sin of envy courses her veins a little too freely. She misled you, I'm afraid, for her gain and, regrettably, your peril."

"Why? What did she hope to gain?"

"I imagine the title of duchess. She may have ended our betrothal, but once she realized another woman would become my wife, the challenge likely reignited her interest." He lowered his voice to a whisper. "You are much more suited to the title."

The weight of all that transpired in the last few weeks slid from the top of Willa's exhausted head to the bottom of the slippers that cradled her tired feet. When James rescued her from the evil Sir Lawrence, she realized she could run no more.

What was the point in running now? The contract remained in place despite the sordid details. Her resolve to continue the fight had been replaced by a growing warmth in her heart toward the man she'd sworn to loathe into eternity.

Tell me you love me, and I'm yours forever, she prayed, breathing into his collar. The familiar scent of citrus and earth mingled together, evoking memories they shared before in close proximity.

James brushed a gentle kiss across her forehead. His lips moved to her temple, then traveled down along the side of her cheek, where he dotted her skin with soft kisses. Willa swayed beneath his touch, anticipating his lips finding hers. He leaned forward, touching their foreheads together. His mouth hovered above hers.

"Why me?" she murmured. James could have any woman, including Lady Genevieve, regardless of her underhanded behavior. Unlike Willa, she possessed vast wealth, a notable title, and a polished exterior.

"Why *not* you?" James whispered. "You are loyal to your family, even to your detriment. You are more accomplished than most ladies with whom I am acquainted. Your passionate nature keeps me on my toes and humbles me where I have been a wretched fool." He pressed his lips to her ear. "End my agony, Willa. Be my wife."

Blood pounded in her brain. She trembled at the eagerness with which she desired to give him her hand and her heart. Her thoughts spun at his pleading.

But her conversation with Sir Lawrence resurfaced, reminding her that James sought monetary satisfaction, not love. Once he'd married Willa, the debt to Sir Lawrence would be satisfied. He didn't desire her because of love. She represented a means to end her father's lack of judgment.

Resistance was utterly futile. If James could not marry her for love, she would marry him for *her* family, as her mama had done when she married Willa's father.

She lowered her head in surrender and stepped back. Unable to speak, the duke's last words burned inside her as she ran back inside. *End my agony, Willa. Be my wife.*

CHAPTER 14

Moonlight bathed the terrace in shifting colors of slate and yellow. Her mother's favorite roses cast a silvery light under the navy blue sky. The night before the presumed wedding had arrived, an intimate celebration dinner marked the impending end of Willa's unmarried status and new adventure as a duchess.

She breathed in the soft scent of flowers blooming along with her feelings. In a short time, she had fallen into a deep, nonsensical love for the man who bargained to marry her. Since her London visit a few days prior, James had stayed closer to her than he had since they met, only leaving her side as dictated by propriety.

Their conversations maintained the height of civility but without the usual banter. James no longer taunted her into an emotional response, plump with provocation. Instead, his responses remained perfunctory and concise, wholly ignorant of the shift in her heart and the details that Sir Lawrence had disclosed.

Her fingertips found a rose petal in the darkness. As she gently pressed it between her thumb and forefinger, she contemplated her decision. The night James returned from London, he had not told her he loved her. Yet, his actions contradicted the notion that he married purely for monetary endeavors. If that had been the case, James would not have cared that she'd uncovered Sir Lawrence's part in the ruse or raced to London to salvage her virtue. Moreover, he would have married Lady Genevieve.

"Dearest cousin, won't you come inside? Aunt Rosamunde has suggested a game of charades to increase the festive atmosphere." Cassandra appeared at her side, rolled her eyes, and laughed. "You must come in and save me from her torture."

Willa forced a carefree laugh, but the amusement didn't reach her eyes. She followed Cassandra into the drawing room, where the family gathered.

"Ah, there's my vision of loveliness." Middleton raised a glass. "Let's make a toast, shall we? To my Wilhemina, the new Duchess of Heighbury, come tomorrow morn!" Her father and aunt beamed.

"And to my dear late Phillipe, may he rest in peace," Aunt Rosamunde added with an unladylike slurp.

Cassandra gasped, pulling Willa aside. "Have you accepted him then, Cousin?"

"It seems I have."

"Why didn't you tell me?" She sank onto a nearby sofa and grasped Willa's hand.

"I only decided this morning, and I needed some time to ponder the enormity of the situation. Circumstances have changed. *I* have changed. My heart, that is." She cast her cousin a weary glance. "After much reflection and the vicar's reassuring prayers, it is my duty as a loving daughter to *both* my parents, in Heaven and on earth, to honor them with this marriage."

Cassandra patted her hand. "This is where you belong.

From a lady to a duchess." She sighed at the daydream. "Your mama would have been most pleased with your choice, Willa. And your beloved papa. Perhaps this will warrant a change in his risky behavior."

"I cannot say. But, I hope he will change course."

Willa's gaze traveled to her father, his cheeks rosy and bursting with gladness. After a long, troubled night, she had requested a private meeting with him after breakfast. While she did not reveal her visit to London, she declared her understanding of their grave situation. Now that she had seen what sort of brute her father had engaged with this regrettable business, she had no desire to jeopardize their home further. He need not be exposed to the man again.

"But are you pleased, Willa?" Cassandra's question interrupted her thoughts.

Her lips parted, but wine glasses raised and clinked, interrupting her response. She watched James from her peripherals. He toasted but remained silent in a corner, never making eye contact with his soon-to-be family.

Her heart ached to see the laughter behind his eyes as he teased or challenged her to a duel of words. To drink in the sparkle of his warm eyes would satisfy a thirst that water could not offer. With his dispirited state, she had concluded that he was no longer happy at the thought of marrying. Once again, she doubted the sincerity of his motives. In the end, he would either follow through with the agreement or risk financial loss.

"How about a game of whist?" Aunt Rosamunde chuckled and then hiccupped, having indulged in too much wine. She covered her mouth with a gloved hand and giggled. Willa cringed at her aunt's disdainful behavior that matched her papa's ridiculousness. Leaving behind his foibles with drink offered Willa a welcome relief in spite of the devotion to her father.

She rose to her feet, making her way across the room to confront James and assure him she now freely accepted their betrothal. Her father promised to relay the news that afternoon to the duke, but she hadn't had an opportunity to gauge his reaction.

As she neared him, he stood and announced he was retiring to bed. Her aunt, father, and cousin must have neither heard nor noticed his proclamation, for none responded. Without so much as a polite bow, he quit the drawing room and muttered a good night to all.

Willa hurried after him, but her shorter legs were no match for his long strides. As he leaped the steps two at a time, a letter slipped from his pocket and fluttered to the base of the stairs.

Willa reached for it and called for him, but he had already disappeared.

I'll give this to his valet. When her glance noted the return address of London, she paused and sank on the steps.

Her mother had taught her never to invade a person's privacy, but curiosity compelled her. Unfolding the letter and documents, it took only moments to comprehend James's demeanor.

Her hands shook, realizing what he had done, and Willa pressed the letter to her heart.

* * *

SLEEP ELUDED James well after midnight. He donned his trousers and paced the floor. Since receiving the revised papers, he had failed to arrange a meeting with his presumed father-in-law with the new agreement.

Running his hands through his hair, he lamented what to do next. First thing in the morning, he would sign the papers and have Middleton do the same. It was the only way. He would never allow Willa or her aunt to be without a roof over their heads. He would ensure they would be provided for, even if it cost him his home at Heighbury Manor.

Would Willa believe his intentions? Her expression was difficult to discern, as usual. She either burned with fire or cooled like ice. He'd take the fire any day over the cold chill of her indifference.

It must be done now.

Determined to release his bride from eternal sadness, James grabbed his jacket, reaching for the letter that contained her freedom.

He shook his cloak and emptied the pockets. "This cannot be. I've had it on my person since its arrival," he seethed.

Lighting a candle by the desk in his room, he began tossing items about in full frenzy. After several minutes inspecting every inch of the room, he concluded he must have left it below in one of the rooms.

He slipped out quietly, easing downstairs as quickly as his feet would carry him. When he was certain he was alone, he entered the drawing room and searched until his hands came up empty. He repeated his search until no satisfaction was to be had.

"So this is the recompense for my greed and selfish motives. My actions have now touched the innocent life of another. Almighty God, have mercy on me for my most disgraceful love of money and land at the cost of another's peace." He paced the floor, remorseful of his motives, and bowed his head in a desperate prayer.

CHAPTER 15

Willa woke with a start. A terrible throbbing head set her on edge as she pulled the blankets tighter. In just a few hours, she was expected to become the Duchess of Heighbury, save for James's intention to liberate her from their matrimonial ruse. Slumber had overtaken her quickly the evening before once she realized he had no plan to force her to marry after all.

She ought to feel relief and gratitude. Instead, butterflies occupied her midsection. To allow James to reveal the plan, Willa kept quiet about the revised contract and letter she'd found. When he was ready, she knew he would disclose all.

The pounding didn't stem from a headache. Someone was knocking on the door.

"Who is it?" she croaked, pulling the covers to her chin.

Cassandra peeked her head inside the door. "The doctor is here to see you, Cousin. He arrived early on the carriage."

"Oh. Send him in then." Willa's lips formed a thin line as she prepared her mind to accept his verdict.

The robust elderly man's breath wheezed in his hurry to

find Willa. After a few moments of examination, he patted her arm.

"Miss Middleton, I have some news. I could not wait until you were married to inform you. After your last appointment, I met with medical colleagues to discuss your situation. We all concur that you do not have palsy but a condition that mimics the same symptoms. Have you observed other family members with the same tremors?"

Willa pressed her forefinger to her temple. "On occasion, my mama exhibited some similar quivering. Looking back, I had worried maybe she had the start of palsy too. Maybe she was only restless, and tending her garden steadied her."

"Or maybe like her, it was also about diet." Dr. Martin beamed as he explained the hereditary condition.

Willa swallowed. "Are you quite certain?"

"You do not exhibit the exact trembling or paralysis of someone with palsy. With this information on your mother, I believe we can put it to rest."

Willa sat up and threw the covers back.

"Careful there, miss. The situation is not dire, and you must eat more meat and a hearty breakfast. I believe your diet to be the culprit. But that does not mean that you must not remain vigilant. If any of these symptoms change or worsen, you must send for me immediately." He sighed contentedly. "However, I believe it is safe to say that you are fit as a fiddle for your nuptials. I shall call on you again when you are home from your honeymoon." A smile spread across his features, revealing a broad gap between his yellowing front teeth.

Cassandra clapped her hands together, thanking the Lord for His providence. "This is so wonderful, Willa! We must ready you for your wedding now."

The doctor leaned in, peering over his spectacles. "My dear, aren't you pleased with my summation?"

Willa cleared her throat. "I thank you, sir, for this most welcome news. I could not be happier." She gulped the air, stalling as a burden slipped from her shoulders and another overtook her senses.

Aunt Rosamunde and Willa's father rushed into the room, having just discovered that the doctor had arrived. After quickly elaborating on his findings, they laughed and hugged Willa tightly.

"What glorious news! We must prepare you. Mr. Brown will be waiting at the church to perform the nuptials." Aunt Rosamunde scurried around the room, preparing the gown Willa would wear to meet her bridegroom. "Gentlemen, please leave us now. Cassandra and I have a bride to dress."

* * *

JAMES PACED the drawing room and tapped his foot in expectation at each corner before continuing his step. He sent for Middleton not twenty minutes before. After waking from the couch where he'd spent the night tossing about, he was taken aback when the man appeared in the doorway whistling a tune and dressed in his Sunday finest.

"Good morning, Your Grace," he chirped. "What a beautiful day we have for a wedding. The fog is lifting, and I daresay I caught a glimpse of the sun. I do believe the Lord Himself is smiling down on us today." He poured himself a cup of tea the maid brought in and offered James a cup.

James shook his head. "Sunny outside it might be, but in here we have a stormy situation."

"What can you mean? Your bride is at this very moment readying herself for the ceremony. She dresses as we speak." His eyes moved over James's appearance. "I daresay you ought to do the same."

Caring not how he looked from a sleepless evening, James crossed the room in two steps and towered over Middleton. "I cannot continue with this charade. Just seven days ago, my lawyer sent the newly revised contract releasing your daughter from any obligation to marry me."

"Good heavens." Middleton's hand shook, and his teacup rattled the saucer as he set it down. "I was supposed to relay the news yesterday but could not find the right moment. Willa has most amicably agreed to the nuptials. I assumed you would be as eager as she to proceed with the vows."

"We spoke about this before, sir. I promised to release her from her duty of the first contract yet bind you to yours in selling the parcel. I do not require repayment for the monetary debt I settled for you to D'Arby. I have managed it myself."

"Oh? And how is that possible?" Middleton wrung his hands. "I knowingly put my family and home in harm's way, and you delivered me from the situation. Surely you intend to be justly paid."

James approached and laid a hand on his shoulder. "I no longer care what D'Arby has to say about the situation. And I made it quite clear to him recently. But, you, sir, must vow never to touch another drop of brandy or attend the gaming tables ever again. That is repayment enough."

"I see." Middleton sat and scratched his chin. "I have done much thinking and praying on the matter. I will agree to your terms, and I thank you for your kindness. Willa and I had a chat yesterday that we should have had long ago. However, my daughter will be disappointed, you know."

"You misunderstand me. The revised papers have arrived, but now they are missing." James stamped his foot.

Middleton remained quiet for a few moments.

"Well, man? Have you seen them? They have been

securely tucked in my jacket for a week now. Just last night, I reached for them so we could seal the contract— They have disappeared into thin air." His jaw clenched in frustration. "I am in agony. I cannot continue with this pretense any longer."

James gripped the velvet arm of a sofa by the fireplace. This was not the scene he had envisioned on this day. For weeks, he looked forward to building wealth, retaining his home, and gaining a wife.

In becoming acquainted with Willa, understanding her moods and thoughts, he drew pleasure from the effect he had on that blaze behind her eyes. By stoking it with his words, he had served up his heart on a platter for her to spear with a fork and knife.

And now the contract and the accompanying letter in which he had revealed his sacrifice were missing. Admission to the compromise of his identity, home, and life with the only woman to have captured his heart produced a new realization. Anyone could have read the contents by now. He no longer held the upper hand to any element of his life.

"My dear duke, I firmly believe you were to keep your word about marrying my daughter. And that is the one piece of our agreement I must insist we resolve. I hope you changed your mind since you hadn't expressed further intent to pursue the matter. She appears to have changed hers. As such, she is upstairs now in anticipation of being escorted down the aisle."

"What do we do now?" James asked through gritted teeth.

Middleton stood and clasped an arm on James's shoulder. "I suggest you either present the papers, we sign and move forward without a wedding, or....fulfill our original contract and marry my daughter." He tapped his pocket watch. "Time and the vicar await us at church."

As Middleton opened the door to leave the room, he

addressed James again. "Either way, I hope you lift this burden upon yourself by confessing your intention to Willa. She deserves to know the truth."

The door closed quietly behind him. James shielded his eyes as the sun broke through the window, momentarily blinding him.

CHAPTER 16

Willa met her father in the garden. Extending her arms, she twirled slowly, revealing a satin empire dress with lace overlay and delicate cap sleeves. Miniature rosebuds dotted her hair, pulled back with a simple ribbon, and coiled into a loose bun, allowing curls shining like copper pennies to escape down her cheeks.

"Daughter, you are a vision." Middleton leaned in and pressed a loud kiss to her cheek. "Your mama would be so happy." He sniffed, then blew his nose into a kerchief.

Willa's heart warmed. It was the most affection her father had shown since before her mother died.

"It's not too much?" She patted the flowers in her hair. "I fear Aunt Rosamunde and Cassandra went a bit too far with my appearance." She wrinkled her nose, embarrassed yet pleased at her transformation.

"Nonsense. Let's get you to church, shall we?" Middleton offered a partial smile, fidgeting with his top hat.

"Papa, what's the matter? I thought you were exceedingly glad I've accepted the duke's proposal."

"I suppose I am anxious," he responded.

Willa chuckled. "I thought nerves were for the bride and groom." She fastened her bonnet decorated with new ribbon, then took her father's proffered arm. With a free hand, she held an elaborate bouquet of roses from her mother's garden, peonies, and ivy that her cousin and aunt had arranged for her. Tucked deep within the center, a folded letter bore her freedom.

The walk to the church allowed Willa and her father time to relish the walk. They reminisced about her childhood before her mother had died with fond memories of the three of them. She thanked her father for doing his best to provide for her.

The vicar, Mr. Brown, met them outside and inquired of the bridegroom. Middleton's eyebrows raised.

"I do not know, sir. I spoke with him not an hour ago."

"And the witnesses?" Mr. Brown's tone made her flush under his scrutiny.

Willa explained they were a few minutes behind. Her eyes scanned the churchyard for James.

"I'm sure he'll be along shortly, my dear. We are a mite early," said her father.

She dawdled behind as the gentlemen moved into the church.

"Papa, could I have a moment?" She gestured to the cemetery. He squeezed her hand and then followed the vicar inside.

She proceeded down the path to her mother's grave, plucking a rose from her bouquet. She placed it underneath the inscription and wiped a tear from her eye.

I wish that you were here to see me so, Mama. Sending silent prayers and longings heavenward, she failed to hear footsteps on the gravel behind her.

"Willa, I must speak with you."

She stood and met James's somber expression. "Will I do?"

His eyes brightened at her appearance. "Beautiful," he whispered.

Satisfaction flooded through her, and she murmured her thanks.

"May we sit?" He gestured to a nearby bench. She agreed, placing a gloved hand on his arm.

James put his head between his hands and rubbed his temples. "I had a wedding gift for you."

She raised her brows but said nothing.

His shoulders slumped. He appeared so broken and unpretentious, far from the arrogant man she'd first met not a fortnight past.

"A wedding gift? Aren't you supposed to wait until after the nuptials?" Her wide eyes observed his agitated demeanor.

Her bridegroom took her free hand with both of his and kissed the palm of her glove. Willa's lips parted in a slight gasp. The intimacy of the movement sent a searing flash of heat from her hand to her heart.

"I wanted to surprise you before the ceremony," he explained. "But first, I have a confession to make."

Willa drew in a breath. She'd been waiting for him to reveal his sacrificial act. Releasing her from an arranged marriage had been what she'd longed for since the first day of the duke's arrival. But now, Willa understood the last thing she desired was to escape his grasp. James would let her go along with his family fortune if he didn't take a wife by his birthday. He must truly love her.

James gripped his knees. "You were correct in your summation of my character that I am unworthy to be considered an honorable man. Despite what you uncovered in London and my former reputation as a wealthy scoundrel, my intentions in purchasing your father's land and having your hand in marriage were solely to further my wealth and prestige. And to save the rights to my home. Even so, I am prepared to surrender my wealth as Duke of Heighbury. Stipulations from my father's will demand that I marry by my birthday next week, or my existence is transferred to D'Arby. From my actions, I am by all accounts a cad, reprehensible. My actions have been selfish and financially driven to the point that I ceased to recognize myself." He hung his head. "'Tis true that 'the love of money is the root of all kinds of evil.' And I allowed that root to take hold of me at your expense."

Willa gripped her bouquet until petals began to scatter. This was not what she had expected. To reveal such honesty without hesitation further spoke of his fine character.

"James, please allow me to convey my sentiments at once, or I'll burst!" She shook with excitement.

He took her hands in his. "Tell me, my love."

"You are not alone in your folly. My soul is not without blemish. I may not have sinned against you by my own hand but in my heart." She pressed the bouquet to her chest in humility.

"How do you mean? I have forced my greed upon you with the utmost contempt."

With a shaking hand, Willa placed her hand lightly on his cheek.

"I have allowed my emotions to get the better of me with unacceptable words that rolled off my tongue in disrespect. I have been argumentative instead of agreeable. In an attempt to dissuade you from this wedding, I exaggerated my condition. The doctor arrived this morning to deliver the results of his examination."

"Pray, tell me at once what he discovered."

"In his estimation, it is nothing dire. However, I am not quite out of the woods yet. He has requested that I be mindful of these occurrences and record them. But I am assured I have nothing to fear so long as I eat properly."

"That is wonderful news! This makes for the most joyous of occasions." As quickly, his countenance changed, and a cloud passed over his features.

"I have attempted and failed to gain the upper hand. When my dear mama left us, I clung to the only certainty I knew: my home and Papa. You rather shook me up a bit. It was rude of me to react in such hostility toward you, and I am thoroughly ashamed. I have been a harsh judge, yet I am as imperfect as anyone and require grace and forgiveness most assuredly. I should not have lashed out at you so."

"We are both broken indeed. Forgive me," James said, enclosing her hand in his.

"On one condition: that you forgive *me*," Willa said, her eyes misting with gratitude. "I must confess that my perception of you was shaped by an evening last spring in London. I was at a ball for my last Season, and you passed me over for a dance. It was most humiliating."

"I remember," he murmured.

"I'm astonished, Your Grace. Your behavior was quite unbecoming."

"I was quite a bore, wasn't I? Quite absorbed with my affairs that evening and how my future would be affected. I'm ashamed of the slight toward you. But, I'm not the cad you might think. I've contacted my lawyer and had him draw up a new agreement. However, the papers have disappeared." He lowered his head for a moment before taking her hands in his. "You are released from any duty to marry me. You may stay here at Middleton Grange with your father as you desire. I'll ensure that Sir Lawrence D'Arby never darkens your doorstep or mine."

With misty eyes, Willa removed the letter from her bouquet and folded his fingers around the parchment. His mouth agape, he removed the papers slowly and perused them.

"Where did you find them?" His brown eyes widened in astonishment.

"You dropped the letter in the hall last night as I hastened to catch you. You're as swift as a horse up those stairs." She laughed lightly. "Don't sign it, James. You and I had an agreement. And here I am, dressed for our wedding day. Would you really care to spoil it?"

* * *

WHEN SHE SMILED TIMIDLY at him, his heart melted around his feet. Either Willa had lost her mind, or she loved him. He had to know. He needed to hear the words.

"You have my full blessing to remain as you are, unmarried, unless another more suitable match comes along." He pursed his lips and fixed his eyes on the bouquet she held.

Willa snorted, then covered her mouth demurely. "I assure you, Your Grace, no other match would be more suitable than *you* to take my hand. That is if you remain committed to your original agreement with my father."

His smile grew as he moved his gaze up to her face. She had the nerve to joke now. Then that must mean . . .

"Are you insinuating that you now wish to continue with the nuptials?" His hand slid down her free arm and gently encircled her wrist. "Tell me you do not toy with my affections, Willa. I could not bear such a cruel joke." His grip loosened, and his eyes explored hers for sincerity.

She eased her hand away from his grasp.

What was she doing now? The churchyard was not the time nor place for games of the heart.

Willa seized the contract and letter of confession from his free hand and slowly tore them in two.

James took her face in his hands and, hovering his mouth over hers, asked, "Does this mean you will marry me and *willingly* become the Duchess of Heighbury?" He pressed his forehead to hers. "That you will love me as I love you?"

She brushed her lips against his lightly before responding.

"I will," she answered, finally having the last word.

~~THE END~~

THE LAST WORD

I hope you enjoyed reading ***The Duke's Last Word***, Book One in the **Love, Most Ardently Series**!

Would you please take a moment to leave a short review?

Amazon
Goodreads
Bookbub

ACKNOWLEDGMENTS

This dream has been in my heart for more decades than I care to admit.

Writing may appear to be a solitary endeavor but it is not. So many have helped me along the way. If I don't mention names specifically, it is only to be respectful of privacy plus there are too many folks out there. I know who you are. God knows who you are.

First and always, I give thanks to my God for giving me this writing gift. I pray I use it to His glory not mine.

Thank you to my parents who taught me the love of reading and sent me to kindergarten at the age of 3 because I was able to read.

Thank you to my husband for his endless support. We have always supported each other through our entrepreneurial endeavors. I could not do this writing business without him. It is a privilege to be married to a man who understands nurturing creativity.

Thank you to my amazing editor, Christina Boyd. If you write Regency, hire her. Yesterday. She has been kind, honest, timely and so helpful. I appreciate her patience with me as a new author. This book wouldn't be where it is without her insight and expertise. Any remaining imperfections are my sole responsibility.

Thank you to the following groups who have been instrumental in classes, resources, critiques, support, etc.: Faith, Hope, and Love Christian Writers, Regency Fiction Writers,

JASNA, Southern Scribe Society, Georgia Romance Writers, ACFW and Word Weavers.

Thank you to my beta readers and ARC team. Your willingness to read and offer feedback and reviews is more appreciated than you will ever know.

Thank you, kind reader, for taking the time to read Willa and James's story. They will be with you throughout the Love, Most Ardently series. Who knows? They may get a longer story down the road.

ABOUT THE AUTHOR

Sophie Leigh Fox is an emerging author of clean and sweet historical romance with a faith element.

She has been reading since age three and writing since third grade, making up stories while on her backyard swing. Sophie crafts sweet romance with a dash of wit, highlighting the struggle of surrendering a stubborn heart to true love.

She never planned to write historical romance, but her first attempt placed her as a 2021 ACFW Genesis Semi-finalist.

She lives in North Georgia with her husband and three dogs. When she's not reading or writing, Sophie loves exploring God's great outdoors or in the kitchen baking a tea time treat.

* * *

I hope you enjoyed reading ***The Duke's Last Word,*** Book One in the **Love, Most Ardently Series**!

Would you please take a moment to leave a rating or write a short review on Amazon, Bookbub and/or Goodreads?

Sign up on my website for the Sips with Sophie blog and monthly newsletter!

sophieleighfox.com

Keep reading for Chapter One of ***Vying for a Groom***!

ALSO BY SOPHIE LEIGH FOX

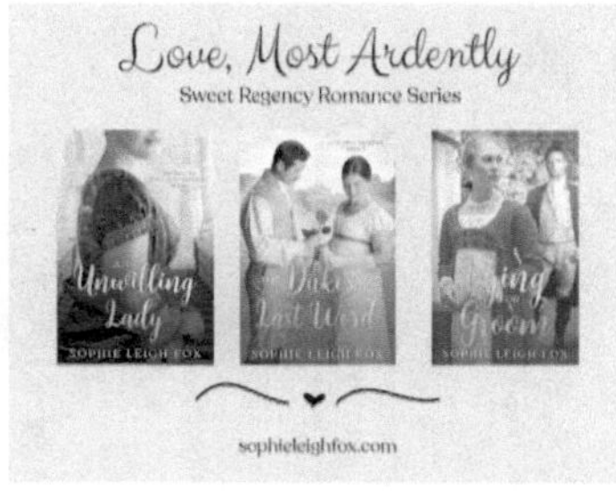

Series Prequel: An Unwilling Lady

Book 1: The Duke's Last Word

Book 2: Vying for a Groom

VYING FOR A GROOM

Love, Most Ardently
Book Two

CHAPTER 1

London, July 1815

THE DELICATE TEACUP slipped from Miss Cassandra Lawton's fingers, spilling tea on the front of her gown, and then broke into pieces on the floor. Dabbing at the fabric with one hand, she stared at the letter in her free hand.

> *Dearest Cassandra,*
>
> *I write to inform you that we have been summoned from our trip to Kent immediately and are for India. As you know, your godfather has been praying for this long-awaited opportunity to best serve as a messenger of the Gospel. Such mission work is the highest calling. My one regret is that it may be years before we are able to return home to England...*

STOOPING to gather the porcelain fragments, Cassandra reflected on how, after her parents had died when she was an infant, her godparents, the Buntlings, took her in. *What am I to do if they are living a world away? Will I ever see them again?*

Even after the adoption, she continued to spend summers with her cousin, Willa, at Middleton Grange to secure a proper upbringing and remain connected to her mother's family.

Her uncle, Sir Edgar Middleton, and his sister, Aunt Rosamunde Livingston, resided at Middleton Grange in Surrey. Cassandra's cousin and Sir Edgar's only daughter, Willa, became the duchess of nearby Heighbury Manor after marrying the duke in the spring. The duchess's late mother and Cassandra's mother were sisters. Even though the Buntlings had formally adopted her, Willa's late mother had remained a motherly influence on Cassandra until her tragic death. On her last visit, Cassandra resided at the Grange until the couple left for their wedding trip to Bath.

Fear for her godparents' safety, mixed with loneliness from their absence, seized the corners of her heart. She shoved the folded paper into the pocket of her gown. Numb from the shocking news, her legs trembled as she ascended the stairs to the bedchamber of Lady Augusta Cromwell.

"There you are. I've been ringing for you for ten minutes now." The white-haired lady perched at her dressing table, waiting for her hair to be styled.

Cassandra clenched her fists, then shook them out. She must remain calm and steady as always. Everyone depended upon her to be the rock in the midst of any storm.

"Do not spill the teacup, dearest." How many times had she heard that in her life, in an effort to keep her sensibilities in check? And so, she had not. Until that very morning.

Cassandra busied her hands, running a brush through Her Ladyship's hair and gently removing any knots. With a practiced hand, she twirled the woman's hair into delicate curls and pinned them efficiently.

Although she had been hired as a companion to the elderly woman, she often served in a dual role as lady's maid when Lady Cromwell's regular maid, Sarah, was occupied with mending.

At one and twenty, her mind wandered to an image of herself twenty years into the future. No doubt age and work would dull her bright blue eyes to gray and fade her reddish-blonde ringlets into colorless strands.

Would Lady Cromwell still be alive?

Unwittingly, Cassandra dropped two hairpins.

"Upon my word, you are behaving strangely today. Are you ill?" Lady Cromwell asked without a hint of severity. She turned her head side to side, admiring Cassandra's handiwork.

"I beg your pardon, milady. I received news prompting me to depart for Surrey if it is not too much trouble. Now that my cousin has returned from her wedding trip, she might console me. She is my closest relation, you know." She caught Her Ladyship's eye in the looking glass.

Lady Cromwell faced her. "Now? What is this news that requires your immediate departure? It has been mere weeks since you returned from the duchess's wedding. The Worthingtons' ball is approaching, and I simply cannot do without you again. I'm expected to visit my sister-in-law in Brighton again next month. Last August was barely tolerable with that horrid Swiss maid she employs. Not to mention the absolute monstrosity of what she calls *le petit déjeuner,* like the French. Do you realize they have dessert for breakfast? How on earth can one be expected to perform their daily tasks without proper sustenance?"

She paused when Cassandra pressed the back of her hand to her mouth, suppressing a sob.

"My dear, what on earth are you about?" The woman reached out to Cassandra with a comforting touch.

Cassandra had been truly grateful from the first day she'd landed her position as Lady Cromwell's trusted companion. At one and sixty, her employer struggled to walk with a cane and needed an able-bodied companion to aid her with her social appointments. Her husband served as a member of Parliament and was often otherwise engaged.

Both her master and mistress were amiable but austere about work and duty. Cassandra kept her head down, standing far from the gossip of the lower servants. At times, she knew she'd been the subject of their chatter. She surmised that Sarah was the source of much of the whispers. Lady Cromwell often praised Cassandra's skills whilst expressing her discontent with Sarah.

She didn't mind the jealousy. The need for a steady position kept her resolute. In return, she earned the implicit trust of the Cromwells.

Unable to articulate a response to Her Ladyship's question without bursting into tears, Cassandra handed her the letter from her godmother. The woman's eyes examined the contents, and her brows knitted together.

"Oh, you poor dear. Now I understand. How distressing for you. While I applaud the Buntlings' charity and Christian service, their sacrifice must rob you of parental and spiritual guidance." She sighed and lifted a vial of hartshorn from her dressing table. After taking a long inhale of the potent solution, she steadied herself. "Of course, Lord Cromwell and I are most obliged to offer our assistance. I'll have a carriage take you to Surrey first thing tomorrow. I'll send an express to Heighbury Manor immediately."

Before Cassandra could protest, Lady Cromwell summoned the housekeeper, ordering the travel arrangements.

Cassandra sighed with relief. Her Ladyship was far too benevolent, but her kindness was the main reason she refused to find another station. Gathering her wits, she finished styling Lady Cromwell's hair, then removed herself to her room in the guest wing and prepared to pack.

As she pondered the inconvenience she might cause the newly wedded couple, another face from Middleton Grange invaded her thoughts. Blue eyes and jet black curly hair. The same face she'd known since childhood comforted her.

Charlie.

They were married years before in the rose garden at Middleton Grange. As children, that is. Willa tortured Charlie into portraying a groom with Cassandra as his bride. He helped place a crown of wildflowers upon her head, then kissed her cheek to seal their make-believe vows.

If he really were her groom, she would not feel quite so abandoned.

After a long sleepless night filled with fervent prayers for her godparents' safety, Cassandra found herself in the carriage heading for Heighbury Manor at dawn's first light.

* * *

Brighton

Sir Raleigh Burgess, Baronet of Burgess Hall, waited as his valet, Biddle, finished the touches on his naval uniform and studied the movements of a swallow landing on a large tree outside. He grew impatient as Biddle styled his hair. Since arriving home the day before, he'd barely had a moment to visit with his mother.

He winced as he came down the stairs, annoyed with the

new hitch in his right hip, a painful reminder of his wartime service to King and Country.

Upon his entering the drawing room, his mother looked up. "There you are," Lady Burgess said, turning her cheek so he might bestow a dutiful kiss.

"How is your afternoon, Mother?" Raleigh asked, sitting and taking the cup of tea offered to him.

"Always the same. Missing your dear father." Her silver hair covered in black Belgian lace, she turned toward the window and sighed.

Raleigh cleared his throat before speaking. His parents had been content in their arranged marriage, but he had never witnessed anything more than a comfortable relationship. After his father's passing, his mother had been lost in her own troubled waters, unable to find peace or purpose.

Raleigh had been serving in the Royal Navy and returned home briefly. He'd been away for these five years since his father's death. Due to the injury he incurred in battle, he expected to be pensioned off and settle permanently in Brighton soon.

"Mother, I believe I shall head to Heighbury Manor and visit with my old chap, James. Do you remember him? We attended Eton together. Didn't you mention in one of your letters that the duke attended Father's funeral?"

"Yes. And the duke and duchess both died not long after your father. Such a pity. So much death. I thank the Heavens you have come home to me whole and complete. Why must you go away again?" Sighing, she closed her eyes and leant back against the divan cushions. "When do you leave for Heighbury Manor? Your aunt and uncle arrive from London next month. 'Tis a shame you shan't be here for their visit."

He could hear the disappointment in her solemn tone. "Day after tomorrow. I thought it might be diverting to visit James."

She turned her sunken blue eyes on him. "I hear he was married last spring. Did you know?"

"Married?" Raleigh set his teacup down. "I say! That is wonderful news. Whomever did he find to be the Duchess of Heighbury?"

Lady Abigail waved her handkerchief. "I am not familiar with the family. Her father is a Sir Middleton, I believe. I don't know the details. Only a bit of gossip."

"If she captured James's heart, I assure you she is not beneath him in what matters most." He beamed and turned to the window, remembering the last time he'd seen his friend. Raleigh had been on his way to join his ship. "Good for him. He was always like an older brother to me."

"Then you can count his wife being like a dear sister." She sniffed. "I would be even more affectionate should you bring me home a suitable daughter-in-law."

He sighed. He wished that he could tell her what she longed to hear.

"Now go and prepare for your trip. I am much accustomed to your departures rather than your arrivals."

Raleigh's conscience reproached him. He hated leaving the dear lady yet again. Aside from family, she rarely received callers and kept herself isolated from Society. But he did want to see James.

"I promise not to prolong my visit to the duke, Mother. Now that Napoleon is defeated and I am officially pensioned off, I look forward to settling down on dry land."

"Oh, I am so relieved to hear it."

He kissed her cheek again and left her to her musings.

Anticipation quickened his step as he imagined bringing a wife home to Burgess Hall. Perhaps that would be exactly what his mama needed to cheer her up, news of his impending nuptials. If only he could be certain of his feelings and the woman in question.

He ran his thumb over the watch in his coat pocket and thought of the blonde lock of hair hidden within. Mistake or not, his steadiness of character could always be prevailed upon in the midst of rough waters.

It won't be long now, Mother. Soon, you will have the daughter-in-law you so desperately wish for.

* * *

SURREY

"MY DARLING, I'm so distressed at your news." Wilhemina, Duchess of Heighbury, rushed forward, pulling her cousin into a comforting embrace.

"Oh, but I regret intruding on you so soon after your wedding, but I needed your sisterly support," Cassandra said as her cousin led her up the front steps of Heighbury Manor.

"It is no imposition at all. The journey *here* was not too taxing on you, I hope." They entered a well-appointed salon near the back of the house where Willa entertained her female guests.

"I would have traveled to Middleton Grange, but your papa is traveling."

Her cousin clucked her tongue. "Too true. I suspect he and Aunt Rosamunde shall not return for the summer. The trip north will do them both good."

Willa rang for tea, then turned to Cassandra. "Now, tell me how I can help you?"

Cassandra's eyes brimmed again with tears. She shook her head. "I do not know. I shall miss them terribly. I fear for their lives, you know. Now I feel foolish for coming all this way to cry like a baby to you."

She hated bothering her cousin, but she truly felt lost.

The news had come so suddenly of her godparents' departure, to be surrounded by family was a lift to her low spirits.

"There are a few of my personal belongings and documents they asked me to secure." She listed her adoption papers and christening gown among the items.

"Surely the church will have received instructions. Have they sent word about a replacement for Mr. Buntling?"

"I received this letter and nothing more," Cassandra murmured, removing the wrinkled paper from the pocket of her gown. She passed it to Willa as the maid returned with a tea tray. "Perhaps the duke could yield some assistance. It has all come about so suddenly... I'm certain my godparents were much surprised as I was at their sudden summons by the Society for the Propagation of the Gospel. We had not expected a mission call to happen so quickly after they applied."

"I will have James take care of contacting the appropriate parties to retrieve any of your personal effects. Do not worry, my sweet. Trust him to handle everything."

Cassandra sat numbly, sipping her tea. Usually, she was the calm and rational one, whilst her cousin required a steady hand to keep her passions in check. Her thoughts traveled again to the perils of her godparents' mission work, and her cup rattled against the saucer. Remembering her cousin's previous battle with undiagnosed shaking limbs, she turned to her.

"And how are your tremors, Willa? I beg your pardon. I should have inquired the moment we sat. Did you find taking the waters beneficial?" Her brow furrowed. Her cousin's mysterious ailment had caused the family alarm briefly before her wedding.

"I honestly cannot say. However, I have not even tripped over my feet since we returned from our wedding trip. James makes sure of that." She patted Cassandra's arm.

"And where is your doting husband?" She offered a weak smile, attempting to divert the conversation away from her melancholy.

Willa's cheeks turned rosy, and her lips parted slowly. "He's out riding." She gazed out the window, scanning the landscape.

"You should have accompanied him. I could have waited here for you to return."

Her cousin waved her hand. "Nonsense. There is nowhere I'd rather be than here with you."

And Cassandra was relieved when she found Willa waiting to greet her in the courtyard upon the carriage's arrival. Her cousin's happiness in marrying the duke had been Cassandra's joy. Since the nuptials in May, Willa's character seemed to have changed immensely from excitable and agitated to serene and content.

A knock at the door interrupted her thoughts, followed by the housekeeper.

"What is it, Mrs. Stern?"

"Begging your pardon, Your Grace. Cook has requested a substitution for dinner that requires your approval."

Willa offered a kind smile, then rose from her chair. "I'll tend to this matter. Cassandra, why don't you greet James at the stables when he returns? You can apprise him of your situation. He will be most pleased to see you."

As she approached the door, Willa turned and added slyly, "Perhaps Charlie can keep you company whilst you wait for James."

CONTINUE READING

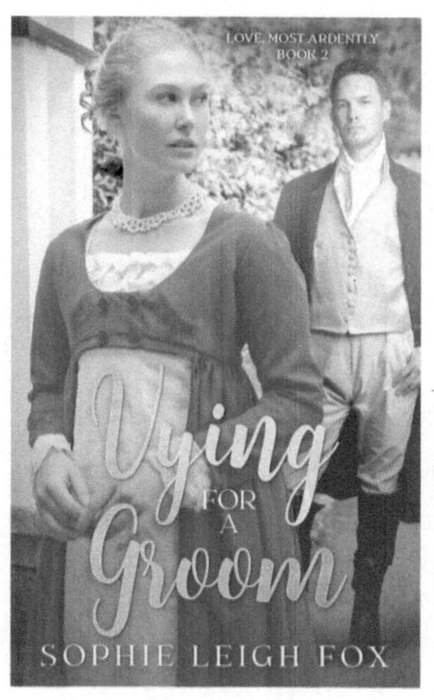

Available at your preferred digital retailer: books2read.com/u/b6EZPp

www.ingramcontent.com/pod-product-compliance
Lightning Source LLC
La Vergne TN
LVHW090526110826
845146LV00003B/1002

* 9 7 9 8 9 9 0 1 2 8 1 2 5 *